GUILTY OR KNOT

MAPLE SYRUP MYSTERIES 12

EMILY JAMES

Editor: Christopher Saylor at www.sayloriting.wordpress.com/services/

Cover Design: Deranged Doctor Design at www.derangeddoctordesign.com

Published August 2019 by Stronghold Books

Ebook ISBN: 978-1-988480-39-8; Print Book ISBN: 978-1-988480-40-4; Large Print ISBN: 978-1-988480-55-8

A Sampling of Murder (Coming Soon!)

For Ezra. You're years away from being able to read—let alone read this series—but one day you'll be able to look back and know your aunt loves you.

A half truth is a whole lie.

— YIDDISH PROVERB

1

When I'd imagined what would go down in our personal history as Mark's and my biggest argument, I'd always thought it would be about criminals.

In my imagination, it was about me wanting to be part of a dangerous case. Or us disagreeing on whether or not the person was innocent. Or even that I was spending too much time working.

I hadn't expected our biggest argument to be about the gender of our baby—or, more specifically, whether we should find out ahead of time whether we were having a boy or a girl. But when the doctor said my upcoming twenty-week ultrasound would be our chance to find out, Mark and I had answered at the same time. Differently.

He'd been quiet the whole walk back to the car.

Mark slid the parking stub into the automated exit machine, and the pole lifted, allowing us out of the hospital parking lot.

The silence made me feel like I had an itch I couldn't reach.

I rested a hand on the barely noticeable stomach mound where our baby slept—or whatever babies of this age did in the womb. I imagined him or her napping, anyway. The doctor said our baby was the size of an avocado now and growing fingernails. "I don't like surprises."

"This isn't a regular surprise." His voice was more clinical than angry. "It's not like I'm planning a trip you'd rather have input on. Knowing won't change whether it's a boy or a girl."

"If we knew, we could stop calling it an it, like the baby isn't a human being yet."

I knew that argument would score a point in my favor. Mark had always said that, medically, the point when a baby became alive and human was at conception. There wasn't any other moment that medical science could point to as the spot when an unborn baby went from being not human to human, or not alive to alive. I agreed with him, but it didn't bother me the way it bothered him to call a baby an *it*.

"We could give the baby a nickname instead," he said. "Elise did that. Arielle was Peanut and Cameron was Little Bean."

Point for Mark. And for Elise. That was an adorable idea. "I still wouldn't know what color to paint the bedroom."

"Paint it yellow and green. Those are neutral colors, right?"

I screwed up my face like I'd eaten a moldy grape. "I've never liked the neutral pastels that everyone seems to think are good baby colors. They look faded."

Mark turned in the opposite direction from home.

He wasn't going to drive us in circles, was he? It was his default, the way some people paced when they needed to think.

He took another turn, and I spotted the cotton candy-pink sign for Brain Freeze, the drive-thru ice cream place that was only open from Memorial Day to Labor Day.

I'd been craving a scoop of their pineapple cream cheese ice cream since March. Mark had promised me we'd go as soon as they opened. And even though we were technically fighting, he'd remembered.

It almost made me want to give in and let him have his way. Almost.

"It's not one hundred percent," Mark said as we pulled up to the screen to give our order. "Sometimes they make mistakes in reading the ultrasound, and we could have an even bigger surprise when the baby turns out to be the opposite gender of what we expected."

"The odds of that happening are infinitesimally small compared to the hundred percent certainty that we won't know the gender if we don't ask."

Mark gave our order into the human-sized ice cream cone, and we sat in silence again as we waited for our treats.

What we wanted was diametrically opposed. For one of us to

get what we wanted, the other would have to sacrifice what they wanted.

The teenage girl at the window handed us our cones. Mark pulled over into a parking space and rolled down the windows. The air carried the scent of fresh earth and things growing. It wouldn't be until late June that the sun started to get hot enough to scorch the life out of the air here in Michigan. In Virginia, it'd already be too hot to be outside long.

This year, I actually appreciated the cooler Michigan temperatures. The baby seemed to have turned up my internal thermostat.

I licked a drizzle of the burnt caramel sauce on my cone and closed my eyes. Only Stacey's assurances that the nausea would pass had gotten me through my first trimester when nothing seemed to settle well in my stomach. Now was supposed to be the time when I could enjoy being pregnant, whatever that meant. I didn't want to spend it arguing with Mark.

Maybe the situation didn't need to be black or white. Most situations had a compromise that could work if you thought about it long enough. That middle ground meant no one got exactly what they wanted, but usually both parties could be content with the solution if they chose.

I indulged in another big lick of ice cream. "What if the doctor told me the gender, but I kept it a secret?"

One of Mark's eyebrows arched. "You think you could keep it a secret from me for another five months? If you're thinking about the baby as a boy or a girl, you'll slip up when you're talking one day, and then I'll know."

Ugg. He was probably right. Not only was I terrible at keeping secrets from him, but not being able to tell meant I also couldn't paint the baby's room. As soon as he saw the color, he'd know.

My cell phone rang in my purse, and then it stopped and started to ring through the car speakers. Anderson's name flashed on the screen on my dash.

We had a meeting scheduled for tomorrow to talk about another pro bono case he was thinking of taking as a favor to his girlfriend. I didn't have a problem with it since the majority of my income came from Sugarwood, and we could have lived on Mark's salary anyway. Providing free legal service to people in need seemed like a good community service to me.

Anderson, on the other hand, still struggled with the idea of giving his time away for free. It didn't fit with the dreams he'd always had for his business.

If a paying client had needs tomorrow, he was likely calling to reschedule.

I tapped the button on the screen. "You're on speaker. Mark's here too."

"Today was the latest doctor's visit, right?" Anderson said. The man never seemed to forget a date or fact. "How's our future lawyer or doctor doing?"

I stuffed ice cream into my mouth to keep from responding

rashly. Anderson meant well, but some days he sounded too much like my dad. My dad was already playing golf with the new young dean of his alma mater so he'd have strings to pull when my baby inevitably followed in his legal footsteps. Anderson at least allowed that the baby might prefer to follow Mark into the medical field. I wanted him or her to have the freedom from pressure to follow his or her own path.

Bleck. Even in my own mind, it was frustrating having to add both pronouns. Mark really needed to let me know the gender.

"The baby's right where he or she should be," Mark said. "Nikki's not gained as much weight as she should, but the doctor thinks she's the one whose lost it because the baby is the right size for the age."

I hid my smile behind my ice cream. Hah. Even Mark was struggling to find ways to phrase things without calling the baby *it*. Maybe all I needed to do was give him time.

The concern in his voice filtered through my self-congratulations. The doctor hadn't sounded like my weight was a huge concern, especially considering how I'd struggled with nausea the first few months. The baby wasn't affected, and that was the important part.

Still, I squeezed Mark's arm and mouthed the words *I'm fine*. It didn't wipe the frown lines off his forehead.

A noise of papers ruffling came through the speakers from

Anderson's end. "I'm glad the report was good because I have more good news for you."

Good news from Anderson could only mean one thing. I silently prayed I was right. I hadn't done more than consult on cases in months. I leaned forward in my seat.

"Our firm signed a new client," he said. "He says he's innocent, but the police are piling up evidence, and there are holes in his case that he can't explain. It has your name written all over it. You interested?"

2

I flashed Mark a *can-we-please* look. We didn't have any other plans for today, but Mark might not want to spend his afternoon driving to my office to look at more case files. Unlike me, he still had to deal with death every day. Today was supposed to be about new life. We should probably spend it looking at cribs or something.

"Has he already been charged?" Mark asked.

Anderson made an affirmative noise. "He's out on bail, and I have the discovery package at the office. He interviewed a few lawyers before settling on our firm."

That spoke to a certain thoroughness and also a level of concern. If he hadn't been worried that the police had something significant against him, he would have hired whoever was cheapest. That definitely wasn't us. Our firm was quickly becoming one of the highest-priced firms in Michigan, and

Anderson still couldn't keep up with the volume of work. One of the things we needed to do before the baby was born was hire a junior lawyer.

"Scale of one to ten," Mark whispered.

"Thirty-seven," I mouthed back.

He shook his head, but he finished off his ice cream cone. "We're on our way."

ANDERSON HAD THE CASE MATERIAL WAITING FOR US IN MY office when we arrived. When I came here, I usually spent my time in Anderson's office, going over files with him, so I hadn't bothered doing much with my office. The upside of that was my desk was clear, giving us plenty of space to spread out.

Mark and I took chairs on opposite sides of the desk. He plucked the medical examiner's report out of the box right away. He flipped silently through the pages rather than putting it back, which told me it wasn't a case he'd worked. If he had, he'd have had to bow out of helping me due to a conflict of interest.

Which begged a question. Why hadn't Mark been the ME called to the scene? "Is this from another county?"

Mark shook his head. "The house where they found the victim's body is in a town about twenty minutes from Fair Haven, but well inside the county lines." He touched a finger to the police reports I'd laid out in front of me. "Look at the date."

I glanced down. December 19. That explained it. Mark and I were gone on our honeymoon.

That was a fairly large gap, though, between time of death and an arrest. Not that arrests always happened quickly. Sometimes months or years could pass between when a crime took place and when the police were ready to make an arrest. That said, the longer the time lapse, the harder it was to close a case. In most of the cases taken on by my parents' firm, an arrest was made within the first couple of months. In this case, we were already over five months from the original incident.

"Anderson made it sound like the police were convinced the client did it, but they moved slowly if that was the case."

"It was originally ruled a suicide by hanging." Mark slid the papers toward me. "Are you okay with looking at pictures?"

Not really, but he wasn't asking if I was emotionally or mentally okay. He wanted to know if I'd lose the ice cream we'd recently eaten if I looked at pictures of the corpse. A valid concern considering how much time I'd spent bent over the toilet the last few months. Crime scene photos had been a struggle for my stomach before I was pregnant.

Things had been better recently, and I wouldn't know until I tried. This was part of my job. And at least with a hanging there wouldn't be any blood.

I edged the photos toward me.

Mark pointed to a close up of the victim's neck. A woman. A dark bruise drew a V in her pale skin.

The back of my throat felt too warm. I needed to focus on it being a puzzle. The ME originally ruled it a suicide and now it was a murder. Thinking about the puzzle was how I'd get through the pictures.

"If she'd been strangled," Mark said, "the bruise would be straight across her neck in a line because her murderer would have been tightening it from behind. A bruise like this one shows the rope was pulling upward on her neck."

I swiveled my gaze away, back onto the police report. I'd seen enough. "Could someone have killed her by hanging her so it looked like a suicide?"

"There weren't any defensive wounds or signs of a struggle elsewhere on her body." Mark turned a few pages. "No drugs in her system, either. I would have ruled it a suicide, too, except that there weren't any rope fibers on her hands."

She'd have had to be a magician to tie a rope without actually touching it.

Mark closed the file. "The ME who filled in while I was away is new. This was his first solo job."

The unfortunate truth of many professions was that people sometimes had to make mistakes while learning. At least this one had been caught in time. Though my client wouldn't think it was fortunate since he said he was falsely accused.

Before I took the case, I needed to be sure he was innocent, and to do that, I needed to first understand why they thought he was guilty.

The start of answering that was how they'd concluded the victim's death wasn't a suicide.

I might be okay with calling our baby an *it* until we gave him or her a name. I wasn't okay with continuing to call the victim a victim. Doing so depersonalized them and desensitized me to the fact that a life had been lost. I never wanted to get hard to death the way my parents had.

I flipped a few pages in the police reports. There it was. Jordan Williams. She was 42 and unmarried.

So how did they decide that Jordan hadn't killed herself?

I gave the rest of the crime scene photos to Mark. I'd need to look them through eventually myself, but my stomach was still touchy after the autopsy pictures.

"It looks like she was hung from the railing in her entryway." Mark held up the photo. I caught the movement in my peripheral vision, but decided not to look up. "She had one of those entryways that's open to the second story."

The image formed in my mind's eye. I breathed in through my nose and out through my mouth. "Did she jump from the second level?"

"No. There's a chair knocked over by where she's hanging."

A chair indicated suicide, too. Or at least that someone wanted it to look like one.

I skimmed the written report of 911 receiving a call from Jordan's brother and the testimony he'd given.

The evidence reports and photos were next. The first picture was a close up of a railing, presumably the one the rope had been tied to. "The scuff mark from the rope wasn't from top to bottom. It was from bottom to top, as if someone hauled her up once she was already tied to it rather than that her weight dragged the rope down as she fell."

That would have been the first tip-off for the police that something wasn't right.

They'd also measured the height of the chair and the height of the victim's body. Based on her height, where she was hanging, and the height of the chair, she'd have had to stand on her tiptoes on the chair. Most suicide victims climbed up on the chair first, then tied the rope around their necks. Very few people would have had the balance to do that while standing on their toes. I certainly wouldn't have.

The knot in the rope was also a complex one, probably chosen for its sturdiness. It'd have been hard to tie while wobbling on your tiptoes.

And yet it looked like a suicide from all other angles. "You said it was ruled a suicide at first. What was the official cause of death?"

"Suffocation. That's consistent with a hanging."

The V mark on her neck proved she hadn't been strangled and then hung, but she'd suffocated. "No fibers in her nose or any sign that she was suffocated by a different method and then hung?"

Mark shook his head.

He'd already said she didn't have any residual chemicals in her system. That crossed off someone drugging her first and then hanging her.

"I guess they could have forced her to climb up onto the chair by holding a gun on her." I couldn't seem to make my voice sound convinced.

Mark's expressive eyebrows rose again. "Would you do it?"

He already knew I wouldn't. There'd been a couple of times where I'd been in a situation where I had to choose, and I'd chosen to go down fighting to make sure that whoever investigated my murder knew it was a murder. Some people might be too afraid and would simply comply with someone with a gun. That said, if they were clearly going to hang you, I had to think most people would prefer to be shot. At least death would be quicker and presumably less painful.

Besides, if someone had a gun on her, that meant two people had to have been involved—one to hold the gun and one to tie the rope around her neck since she didn't have rope fibers on her hands.

What that left us with was a suicide that couldn't have been a suicide and yet didn't seem like it could have been a murder, either.

---

3

*T*he muscles in my stomach tightened uncomfortably. Anderson wouldn't be as careful about whether or not a client was innocent. He'd tell them the one rule—the client had to be honest with us even if they lied to everyone else—but he'd likely take them at their word.

I'd just come out of a case where my client was innocent, but she made everything worse for herself by lying to me repeatedly.

I also hadn't had a choice about defending her. I owed a huge favor. This time, I wanted to be sure I felt comfortable with what I was getting myself into.

I wriggled Anderson's file full of notes he'd already taken out from underneath the other paperwork, looking for the information about our client and what the police had on him. At this point, I didn't even know his name yet.

Anderson's file was thin. That, coupled with the fact that it was full of handwritten notes, told me the newness of this case. Anderson had probably only met with the client once or twice himself so far. Otherwise, there would have been more notes, and they would have been typed. Anderson preferred hand-writing his notes, but our legal assistant always entered them into the computer shortly after.

I skimmed Anderson's notes. "Our client is the victim's brother. Zach Williams."

"Most murders are committed by someone the victim knows," Mark said.

I gave him a *not helpful* head shake. The police worked under the assumption that a victim likely knew their killer, and so did I. Truly random killings were much more difficult to solve because the connections we all depended on weren't there.

That said, just because Jordan was probably killed by someone she knew didn't mean it was necessarily her brother.

Mark leaned over the desk, his gaze on the papers. "What do the police have on him?"

His voice had an eager quality. Mark had helped me with a lot of cases. As much as he enjoyed the puzzle of it the same way I did, he was rarely excited to find out what made a person look guilty.

I leaned back. It was almost like he was hoping Zach was guilty so I wouldn't take the case. "According to Anderson's notes, he found Jordan's body."

Mark mimicked my body language and leaned back as well. "That's hardly something he can be held responsible for."

I ran a finger down the page, finding Anderson's exact words about it. "The police initially suspected him because of how dispassionate he was on the 911 call."

"Could have been shock," Mark said.

It could have been, but experienced police officers could recognize the difference. They'd seen and heard enough shock that their instincts usually picked up on quiet cues, even if they couldn't put it into words.

The skin on the back of my neck felt tight and itchy. The police weren't always right. They were right more than they were wrong, though. Otherwise, I'd have been taking in more cases than Anderson, not the other way around.

I moved my finger to the next point in Anderson's notes. He really did model almost everything off my dad. The first place my dad liked to start in any case was *why do they think our client did it?*

"He also left her hanging rather than trying to cut her down. The responding officer thought that was strange. The instinctive reaction most men have is to get their loved one down in the hope that they're still alive."

Mark nodded. "I've rarely heard of a case where the person who finds the victim doesn't try to free them."

He didn't sound overly eager anymore. He just sounded like Mark.

Maybe I was being paranoid. It wouldn't be the first time. Mark drove me here, after all. He'd helped me look through the files and interpret the medical examiner's findings. He'd been nothing but supportive, so the pregnancy hormones were probably interfering with my ability to read him. Some lawyer version of mood swings.

A case would be good for me. It seemed like my mind was going to start creating puzzles to solve otherwise.

"Do they have anything concrete in the way of motive?" Mark asked.

I glanced back at Anderson's notes. "Their dad recently passed away. He left the house to Jordan rather than to both of them jointly. Zach didn't receive any sort of monetary compensation to make up for it, either. All the money from the estate had already been used up by their dad's medical bills and the other creditors."

Like the bank who held the mortgage on the house.

Ownership of the family home wasn't the strongest motive I'd ever come across. It wasn't the weakest, either. People had killed for a lot less. Anderson's notes went on to say that Zach had extensive student loans and was paying alimony to an ex-wife.

Financial stress didn't make Zach guilty, though.

I'd reached the point where I had questions only he could answer. I'd learned from my past mistakes. I wasn't taking on another client until I spoke with them first and knew exactly what I was getting myself into.

ZACH WILLIAMS COULDN'T MEET US THAT AFTERNOON, SO MARK and I spent the rest of the day shopping for cribs and car seats. By the end of the day, I'd decided I'd much rather investigate a murder than try to decode all the car seat options. In fact, I'd rather repair broken sap lines at Sugarwood or balance our books or pretty much anything other than shopping for car seats again.

Mark had to testify in court the next day, so I drove back to my office alone to meet Zach Williams.

With a name like Zach, I'd created a picture in my mind based on Zach Morris from the old *Saved by the Bell* TV show that was popular when I was a kid. Blond, thin, preppy, cavalier.

The man sitting in the reception area when I arrived was thin, but nothing else matched my mental image. He wore wrinkled scrubs in a pale blue color that looked like it'd gotten that way from repeated washings and the kind of ugly sneakers that people only wore because they were comfortable. His hair was buzzed shorter than most of the Fair Haven police officers. His shoulders had a droop to them that spoke of more than a long day. I pegged him at around thirty-five.

If someone told me he was suspected of murder, I'd have assumed an angel of mercy type of situation.

His gaze flickered almost immediately to my belly. My baby bump wasn't big enough that strangers could accurately tell if I was expecting or not yet. His gaze lingered just long enough to make me think he'd guessed correctly.

He rose to his feet. "Ms. Fitzhenry-Dawes?"

I offered him a hand and a smile. "Nicole. *Fitzhenry-Dawes* can be a bit of a mouthful."

The quasi-joke normally set people at ease. Zach didn't even smile.

"Zach," he said. "Williams."

He added his last name slowly enough that I got the impression he wasn't used to giving it. So he was more likely a nurse than a doctor. Doctors went by their last names, but nurses only gave their first.

I led the way into my office. His gaze did that quick flicker again, like he wanted to assess the situation quickly and without getting caught.

I motioned to the chair Mark sat in yesterday.

Zach didn't move from his position in the doorway. "Are you new to the firm?"

The way he said it reminded me of how medical professionals asked questions that you knew had a deeper purpose, but they did it with an air and tone meant to keep you from suspecting how important your answer was. It was a trick of their trade to keep patients from giving the answer they thought was expected of them or lying because they were afraid the truth would indicate they had something serious.

In this case, my office must be making him concerned that this was my first case. The sparseness of it made it look like I hadn't finished moving in. He must think he'd been pawned off on a newly hired junior associate who would be learning through his case. And a pregnant one at that who'd probably pass him off to someone else if the case took too long and her baby was born.

Only the pregnant part carried any sort of legitimate concern, though he should be more concerned that the pregnancy would knock me off my feet—literally—before the baby was born. With how much my swollen feet ached right now, all I wanted to do was go home and soak in a warm tub.

I settled into my chair. The ache in my feet eased. If I could prop them up on something it'd be even better, but that definitely wouldn't look professional or instill confidence in Zach.

Part of the reason Anderson agreed to a partnership where I only consulted or worked cases where the client was innocent was because of the cred my last name carried. As much as it made me feel a bit like a freeloader to keep leaning on what my parents had done, I couldn't effectively work a case where my client didn't trust my abilities.

"I'm a new partner to this firm, just since I moved to

Michigan. Before that, I worked for Fitzhenry and Dawes in Washington, DC."

If Zach had done his research the way it'd sounded like he had, that should connect the dots for him. Any search for top criminal defense attorneys turned up my parents' firm, regardless of where you lived.

Zach slid into the chair. "I thought your name sounded familiar. What brought you to Michigan?"

The question sounded natural enough, but there was that underlying sense to it again that I was being examined. Like what he really wanted to know was whether Michigan was exile because I'd screwed up in DC.

Not every client would trust me from the start. Especially not if they met Anderson first. He had the same air as my dad. The one that every quarterback and CEO also had, where they walked into a room and generated their own gravitational force.

The little voice in the back of my head that still liked to pop up from time to time and try to tell me I'd never be as good a lawyer as they were whispered seductively in my ear.

Shut up and let me work, I told it. *Sometimes being underestimated is an advantage.*

I gave Zach my most confident smile and prayed it reached my eyes. I had a suspicion that he'd notice if it didn't. Zach seemed to smell potential weakness the way dogs and bees could smell fear. "My Uncle left me some property, and I fell in love with the area." I lowered a hand to my stomach. "And with my husband. He works for the county."

Zach shifted, letting his back finally touch the chair. I had him—at least for the moment—which meant we could finally get down to business.

I stretched my hand toward my briefcase where I had his files. I didn't want him to misinterpret my next statement as a sign that I knew nothing and was playing catch-up. "I've read over everything relating to your case, but I'd like to start with hearing about what happened from you. It gives me a chance to ask questions to help me start building your defense."

Not a single muscle moved in his face. "I don't know what I could possibly add."

This case already presented a challenge in the circumstances surrounding Jordan's death. A client who was reticent to talk to me wasn't going to help. Maybe Anderson had made a mistake in handing this case over to me, regardless of whether or not Zach Williams was innocent. Zach clearly had expected to work with Anderson.

Then again, I might be reading too much into it. As a nurse, Zach had trained to keep his expression calm and unbiased. That might actually be why the 911 operator and the responding officer felt his reaction to his sister's death lacked emotion. He was used to holding it in check.

If I looked at it from the angle of his history, he might think he had nothing more to add because he'd tried to be detailed the first time, like when he recorded a patient's vitals. He might not realize that in the legal field, it wasn't only about the facts. It was about how you could spin them, and the police were spinning the facts in such a way as to make him look guilty, whether he was or not.

I'd have preferred to have him tell me the story. When people got talking, they often included details I might not have thought to ask about.

This time, I'd have to lead the way by asking the questions.

"Let's start with what you did when you found your sister." I kept my voice gentle. I had the impression he felt a lot more inside than he showed. That included grief. "Did you try to get her down and resuscitate her?"

I knew he hadn't, but it was the best way I could think of, without showing him my hand, to broach the topic of why he'd left her hanging. In my last case, my client had been lying even though she'd been innocent. This time, I planned to test his honesty a bit before I believed him.

He rested his hands on his knees. It wasn't as relaxed a gesture as if his hands stayed on the arms of the chair, but he also wasn't clenching his hands or tucking them between his legs, either.

"She was beyond that point." He looked off to the side of my face, as if he saw her hanging there behind me. He focused back on me. "I've been an ER nurse for ten years. I know the stages of death. I could have done CPR until paramedics arrived and it wouldn't have done any good. The window had closed. I thought it'd be better to leave everything untouched for the police."

That made sense, but only if he'd thought it might be murder. The inconsistency wriggled around in my brain. "You weren't sure it was suicide?"

He looked to the side again. "There wasn't a note. I didn't want to take the chance."

Only half of all suicides left a note. Most people didn't realize that, though. The common belief was suicides almost always left a note and that no note indicated foul play.

"I thought it would help the police either way if I touched as little as possible," Zach said. "I did take her pulse. Just in case I was wrong somehow. I wasn't."

The detail about taking her pulse contradicted what he'd said about knowing what "too dead to save" looked like. If he'd explained it that way to the police, it would have set off more red flags for them, like he was setting up an excuse in case they found his DNA on her body.

The tricky part for me was figuring out what I believed about him. He might be lying. Or he might have done things that seemed contradictory because—ER nurse or not—finding a loved one dead was a trauma.

Court cases could stretch out for months or years. I might have to be involved with this even after my baby was born, taking time away from him or her. I wanted to be sure I was fighting for an innocent man.

So instead of asking him about the facts, maybe it was time I pressed into feelings and thoughts. Liars often rehearsed their facts—what they saw, what they did. They sometimes even thought to rehearse their motivations—*I didn't do this thing because I was scared*, for example.

They didn't often think to rehearse the less obvious elements.

"What did you think when you first saw her?"

His fingers stiffened. "I was angry at her."

For the first time, the tone of his voice shifted. It hardened in a way that said he was trying not to raise his voice.

Anger was actually a very normal emotion in those left behind by suicide, according to my counselor. She said people used anger as a shield when their grief was too raw to face.

My heart wanted to console him, but I couldn't fill in the blanks for anyone during a murder investigation. I had to sit quietly and wait for him to elaborate.

The clock on my wall ticked out the seconds. Ten. Twenty.

Zach shifted forward in his chair. "Is there anything else you needed to know? I just got off a twelve-hour shift, and I'd like to go home to shower and get some sleep."

Okay, so pregnant pauses weren't going to work with him, either.

And I still didn't have a clear read on him. Worse, it didn't look like I was going to be able to get one. He was too used to holding in his thoughts and emotions. Perhaps all that left me with was the element of surprise.

I stood as if I were going to walk him to the door. "Did you kill your sister?"

It was like he'd been wearing a mask and it cracked down the middle. Anger flashed across his face, as did something else that I couldn't sort out before he closed down again.

"Jordan did this to herself. I told the police that. I told your partner that. She was depressed. She'd been suffering from caregiver fatigue for a long time before our dad died, and then afterward between her grief and the stress at her job, she kept sinking lower. There was nothing I could do to change her mind on things."

Self-recrimination. Maybe that was what I'd seen on his face and couldn't interpret. He was angry at her, but he was also angry at himself. He felt like he should have been able to save her.

Finally. Dealing with him had been like wandering around a maze with a blindfold on. I was still deep in the maze of this case, but at least now the blindfold was off. I could face him more on a personal level since I better understood what was hiding underneath. Being able to make that personal connection had always been my secret ingredient. I didn't know how to function without it.

I moved around my desk to close the distance between us.

"The police have proof that she didn't kill herself." I kept my voice soft and gentle. If I could get him to grasp this one thing today, we'd have made real progress. Once he believed what had happened to his sister, we'd be working together rather than against each other. "We're not going to get you acquitted by arguing that she did. If you don't want to go to prison, then we need to build a case that casts enough reasonable doubt for a jury to vote not guilty."

He covered his face and rubbed his hands up and down. "You're sure," he said between his fingers. "There's no way it could be a suicide?"

My feet throbbed again already. I glanced at my desk, but there was no way I'd be able to perch on the edge gracefully. "None. They're not sure how it was staged, but they do know it wasn't suicide."

He lowered his hands back to his lap. He'd wiped all emotion away from his face. "Then someone from her work must have killed her. She thought something unethical was happening, and she wanted to expose it. I tried to talk her out of it. It's one of the reasons I thought she'd killed herself. The psychological stress on whistleblowers puts them at higher risk of suicide, and she was already struggling. But if she didn't kill herself, then they killed her to keep her quiet."

4

*S*tacey Rathmell, Sugarwood's assistant manager, took the end of the industrial measuring tape and paced away from me across the clearing in our sugar maple bush. She stopped and turned back. I made a silly wave to baby Noah, wiggling all my fingers. He grinned at me from his position strapped to Stacey's front.

Where Stacey went, Noah went. The kid seemed able to sleep anywhere. He rarely even cried in church, and Stacey didn't bother leaving him in the nursery. I'd have to get her to spill her secrets before my baby was born. It couldn't possibly be as easy as she made it look, especially since she was doing it on her own.

Stacey held up her end of the measuring tape. "What are we at?"

I glanced down. "A foot too short still."

We were out in the bush, trying to find a clearing big enough to accommodate a pop-up screen, a refreshment stand, and an audience. Stacey had come up with a fantastic idea for increasing Sugarwood's visitor revenue in the summer months. We were going to show old movies in the woods every Saturday, weather permitting. Fair Haven didn't have a movie theater of any kind, so Stacey thought we'd even get locals coming out along with the tourists.

The location was the problem. The draw to it was that we'd be showing movies in the woods. We needed an easily accessible spot—so that visitors could park and walk in—that was big enough to hold the number of people we needed to make a profit and that also had a spot where we had properly spaced trees in a straight line to anchor the screen.

Stacey motioned for me to wind the tape measure back in. "I think we're going to have to build a framework."

By *we* she meant her and Russ. No one was letting me anywhere near power tools. I wanted to keep all my digits attached.

I finished cranking the soft tape back into its case. Mark and Russ should be finished pacing off the clearing and making calculations for how many people they thought it could comfortably seat. I glanced around to where I'd seen them last.

They stood off at the far edge of the clearing, as if they'd stopped there to talk where they wouldn't be overheard. Russ' hands waved around like he was trying to take flight.

Stacey stopped beside me. "That doesn't look good."

No, it didn't. Mark was angled away from me so that I couldn't see his expression, but Russ was red in the face.

"What's going on?" I called.

Russ glanced in my direction, and the volume of his words went up enough that I could catch the tone but not enough that I could hear what he was saying.

"I wouldn't get in the middle of it." Stacey mumbled the words in that under-the-breath-but-loud-enough-to-be-sure-you-hear-me way that teenagers seemed to have mastered.

There shouldn't have been an *it* to get in the middle of. "What can they possibly be fighting over? How many people we can fit in here before we violate some weird safety code? Are there even capacity limits for open spaces?"

Stacey shrugged. But she also took the measuring tape from my hand and backed away like she was going to measure more spaces.

I couldn't blame her. Since I was buried alive, Russ practically had Stacey and me under house arrest. A couple of times I'd been out walking and I'd caught Stacey taking the long way to the Short Stack parking lot, where she kept her car, rather than walking by Russ' house. If she walked by his house and he spotted her, she'd have to undergo an inquisition about where she was going, who she'd be with, and when she'd return.

Even though I hadn't intentionally gotten myself buried alive, I felt responsible. Stacey was a bit like the younger sister who now had to abide by stricter rules because of her wild older sister's actions.

This time, at least, I could make sure that whatever this was about didn't bleed over onto Stacey. As much as she loved working at Sugarwood, Russ could end up pushing her away—and completely out of his life—if he wasn't careful. Even an event like this that might be over something as simple as Russ freaking out about damage to the grounds was causing her to back away.

I marched over to the other side of the clearing and stopped equidistant between Mark and Russ. Until I figured out the source of the argument, I'd be Switzerland. Well, maybe not Switzerland. Mark had my complete loyalty even when I disagreed with him.

"If chairs are going to be this much of a problem," I said, "we can tell everyone to bring blankets and sit on the ground."

A smile got halfway up Mark's lips. Russ glared at him, and it died before his dimples could show up.

Not good. This wasn't Russ a little bit angry. This was Russ going from mild-mannered Bruce Banner to building-smashing green Hulk angry. You'd have thought Mark took a chainsaw to our young trees with the way Russ was acting.

Humor wasn't going to defuse this situation the way I'd hoped. "What's going on?" I asked again.

They'd ignored me the first time, pretending they hadn't heard. They couldn't ignore the question now.

The wind blew Russ' thinning hair back from his forehead,

making it stand up even straighter than it did when he finger-combed it. "You took on a client."

Was this about stretching myself too thin now that I was pregnant? Russ had barely allowed me to help at all when the sap started running. He'd thought I should rest. I'd had to fight him to let me do even simple tasks.

But the busy sap season was over. There wasn't much for me to do at Sugarwood, even with our plans for Movies in the Woods, as Stacey and I had dubbed it.

Maybe that was it. Even though Russ and I had talked about my plans for the future and he knew I wanted to stay involved with Sugarwood, me taking on a client might make him afraid I'd become less and less involved with Sugarwood as time went on.

My instinct was to go to Russ and put a hand on his arm, but his tight posture had *stay away* written all over it.

I gave him a no-need-to-worry smile. "I'll be working from home rather than from my office most of the time. I'll still be here for anything Sugarwood needs."

Russ' caterpillar-like eyebrows rose up almost to his hairline. "It's not about Sugarwood. You have a baby to think about."

Our baby wasn't even born yet. It went where I went. It wasn't like I even needed to hire a babysitter or have Mark take time off work to care for the baby while I was gallivanting around. The baby was about as low maintenance right now as he or she was ever going to be.

Russ's cheeks quivered, like the emotion in the rest of his body that he was holding in had to find release somewhere.

Real observant, Nik. I gave myself a mental glare. *You should have known what this was about from the start.*

It wasn't about how much time I was spending. It was about how I would be spending it.

"Not every case is dangerous. This came through my firm. Anderson and my parents defend clients all the time without—"

"Without nearly getting themselves killed every time." Russ' words almost sputtered.

I probably would have picked a more diplomatic, soothing way to say it. But that was it in a nutshell.

I couldn't think of anything to say to defend myself. It did seem that, as hard as I tried to stay safe, I ended up in danger. It'd gotten to the point where my counselor asked if I was secretly depressed and suicidal. I wasn't. I didn't want to die, especially now.

When I called my mom after I'd been buried alive, she said I ended up in life-threatening situations because my skills and determination to find the truth made me a threat. She'd actually sounded proud when she said it. She might not like the danger I frequently faced, but she now saw me as strong enough to handle it. And a strong daughter was what she'd always wanted.

Russ clearly didn't share her sentiment. He must have misinterpreted my hiatus from defending clients as a sign that I was quitting because of my pregnancy. I'd never explicitly told him that I wasn't working because innocent clients were rare.

"And you." Russ stabbed a finger in Mark's direction like he wanted to poke him in the chest with it. "You let her keep doing this."

Mark's face went pink except for white lines around his lips. "I don't *let* her do anything. I'm not her boss or her slave master."

Mark's voice had so many layers to it that I wasn't even sure I could peel them all back. I'd never heard him sound quite like that before.

The anger at the front was clear—he didn't like Russ implying that I was under his control. That was probably why he'd tried to isolate the conversation. He knew how I'd feel about even the suggestion that I wasn't capable of taking care of myself.

Mark hadn't had to deal with this version of Russ before, though. I'd never seen Russ lash out at Mark. Ever. I'd faced this Russ a couple of times, and I knew that all of this stemmed from love. Even though I didn't like the implications of his words, I wasn't going to take offense at them. It wasn't that he really doubted my ability. He was just scared.

That under-layer that had been in Mark's voice felt like a cousin of fear as well. We'd had a lot of discussions during our time together about me not taking unnecessary risks. I'd tried—however unsuccessfully—ever since. But now any risky situation I found myself in would put our child in jeopardy as well.

I wanted to promise that this case wouldn't be like the others.

I'd thought each new case wouldn't be like the others. Promising I'd be completely safe wasn't a promise I could make anymore. When your work involved revealing the secrets of people who were willing to kill to get what they wanted, you sometimes did become a target. I didn't like it any more than they did, but what was that quote? The only thing necessary for evil to triumph was for good people to look on and do nothing.

I couldn't be one of those people who stood by and let evil win.

I didn't know what that meant for me once our baby was born. Then I'd also have my responsibility as a mother to protect my child. Could I keep practicing and also keep our child safe?

Right now, I only had one answer I could give. "It's my job, Russ. I'll be as careful as I can doing it, but it comes with danger the same way Elise or Erik's jobs as police officers do. Even Mark's job comes with risk."

I'd only been partially to blame, for example, when we'd ended up upside down in a ditch in December. Mark had been the one everyone wanted to stop that time. His knowledge was the key to figuring out who'd been behind the corruption in the Fair Haven police department for so many years.

"You're not trained like Elise." Russ' cheeks bulged, and he blew out a large puff of air. "Hire a bodyguard at least."

I didn't even want to think about how much a bodyguard

would cost. And how would I even know when I should keep my bodyguard around and when to let them go? Certainly Russ couldn't expect me to have a bodyguard when I was at home.

All of that didn't even touch on the main issue. "A lot of what I do involves talking to people and convincing them to talk to me. I can't do that if I have what amounts to a grown-up babysitter following me everywhere."

"Hey Russ?" Stacey called from behind me.

We all turned.

She rubbed Noah's back. "I'm feeling a little tired. Could you walk us back home?"

She didn't actually lie by saying something like "Noah was up all night," but the implication was there.

Russ' gaze hopped between Stacey and me. Mark moved in and slid an arm around my waist—his subconscious signal to Russ that he'd take care of me.

Russ nodded to Stacey. He gave me a firm look. "I'm not done talking about this."

Thanks for the warning, the snarky part of me wanted to say, *so that I can avoid you.*

As much as his overprotectiveness might make me want to pull a teenaged sneak-out-of-the-window-to-avoid-my-parents move, I wouldn't actually avoid him. Stacey and I were the closest thing to family that Russ had. And even if I hated to admit it, if my Uncle Stan were still around, he might have sided with Russ.

Russ and Stacey headed in the direction of their houses. Other than my and Mark's house, their two homes were the only ones on Sugarwood property.

Stacey shot a glance back over her shoulder that clearly said *I'm taking one for the team this time, but you owe me.*

My heart beat at double-time even after they disappeared into the bush. I linked my hands with Mark's and raised up on my toes to kiss him.

The fierceness in his return kiss sent heat spiraling through my belly and a cold chill down my arms. I pulled back.

He gently tugged me back in and tucked me close.

"Is Russ right?" His heartbeat under my ear made it so that I could barely hear his soft words. "Should I be doing a better job of protecting you?"

See, the nasty voice in my head said. *Even Mark doesn't think you can take care of yourself.*

The voice in my head was so loud that I almost missed that current running deep under Mark's question. It'd been there when he answered Russ as well.

Fear, but something else. Insecurity? Guilt?

My brain clicked the pieces into place. Back before Mark and I were a couple, I'd ended up in a dangerous situation. Mark thought Erik and I were dating, and he lashed out at Erik over it, saying that Erik should have protected me.

I hadn't realized it then, but Mark's reaction had been about me and yet not about me. It'd also been a reflection of the guilt he still felt over his first wife's suicide. She hadn't been able to recover from the loss of their unborn daughter. Mark's head knew it wasn't his fault, but his heart sometimes still tried to tell him otherwise.

Russ' accusation now must have triggered those feelings.

I leaned back enough to be able to look up at him without breaking his hold on my waist. "You can't follow me around everywhere I go. You wouldn't be able to work if you did that."

He rubbed a hand up and down my back, like it helped remind him I was here and real. "And I'm not going to ask you to stop doing the job you love. That's what Russ wants me to do."

That must have been part of the conversation before I got there. Either that or Mark was reading into what Russ said based on their long history.

He let me go, but kept a hold of my hand and turned us back toward our house. "How important is taking this case to you?"

In other words, would I consider not taking any more cases until Russ calmed down.

Tightness pressed down on my chest. I should say *Yes, I'll set this case aside and take it easy*. I should put Russ' feelings ahead of my own, shouldn't I?

But if I didn't take this case, I might not get another chance before the baby was born. I didn't want to be working during his or her first year of life unless it was to quickly finish up a case that went on too long, so this might be my last chance for a long time.

Besides, Russ might never overcome his fears. If I backed down now, he might simply think he'd won and push harder the next time. We might create an unhealthy cycle we could never get out of.

I couldn't live my life based on what Russ wanted any more than I'd been able to live my life based on what my parents wanted. I'd tried living to meet other people's expectations. It hadn't made me very happy. It also hadn't made me very helpful to anyone else.

I met Mark's gaze. Tight, tiny lines framed his eyes.

I might not want to live my life for Russ, but I'd give up this case if Mark needed it. If that's what it took for him to feel secure, I'd give up anything he asked. Not because I had to. Not because he was a man and I was a woman.

Because one thing I saw in all the long-lasting couples around me was that they didn't insist on their own happiness at the other person's expense. They found ways that they could both be content. Those ways were sometimes unconventional and often not understood by everyone around them, but what mattered was that it worked for them.

"Do *you* want me to give up this case?"

Even though I didn't say it, I knew Mark would also understand the unspoken question. Do you need me to stop being a lawyer? It was what we were really talking about here. We had no guarantee that the cases I worked would ever be safe or even safer.

"I'm worried, too, but I knew this was who you were when I married you. You have my support if you want to pursue this. All I've ever wanted is that we make these decisions together."

That's what I wanted, too. Before I met Mark, I never realized how nice it was to have someone to make decisions with.

I had Mark's support. Russ would have to find a way to work through his fear. "This might be the last case I have time for before the baby's born. I want to do it."

Mark tightened his hand around mine and headed us back toward home again. "Then you take the case."

hree days of re-reading everything in Zach Williams' case files hadn't brought me any new revelations, but there hadn't been much I could do over the weekend. I'd had to wait on Hal, the private investigator our firm kept on retainer, to research the pharmaceutical company where Jordan worked.

He normally gave me his reports over the phone, but this time he'd asked that I meet him at our office. He had to be there anyway to deal with a few items Anderson had assigned him for other cases.

I hadn't yet met Hal in person, so it seemed like as good a time as any.

I arrived before they were finished. I should probably wait for Hal in my office, but my feet already felt too big for my shoes, and I had nothing to prop my feet up on in my office. Both Mark and my doctor assured me that swollen feet were normal. Normal didn't mean it was any more pleasant to deal with.

I pulled a second chair over to the one I planned to sit in and settled in with my feet up.

I glanced down. The only drawback was this position made my baby bump bulge out and look bigger than it otherwise did. Even the flowy shirt I'd chosen settled down around it rather than hiding it.

While I waited, I read a few more articles on whistleblowing. They didn't tell me anything all the others hadn't already. Whistleblowing put great emotional stress on people, making them often feel unsafe and increasing their risk for drug or alcohol abuse. All of which pointed back to suicide, and we knew Jordan hadn't committed suicide.

I typed in *murder of whistleblowers* instead. The only even remotely related results that came up were sensationalized lists of suspicious or mysterious deaths of whistleblowers.

I read a couple pages anyway. Most of the deaths were in foreign countries. The only one in North America was the gunshot wound death of Enron whistleblower John Clifford Baxter. Police ruled his death a suicide, despite strange evidence that didn't match up.

At least the police weren't trying to cover up Jordan's murder. While I didn't know anyone in the department who'd investigated her death, they seemed to want the truth. They'd charged Zach because they thought that was where the evidence pointed. My job was to show that, however pure their motives, they were wrong.

The door to Anderson's office opened, and I lowered my feet. The rest was nice while it lasted. I wouldn't get much more this week. Along with following whatever leads Hal found, I needed to finish selecting the movies for the summer with Stacey, source them, and find out where we could buy a movie screen. Stacey and Russ were anxious to start building the frame, but they couldn't until we were absolutely certain we could buy the size of screen we wanted.

I pulled my mind back to the present.

Anderson was coming toward me with a man who had to be Hal.

He was younger than I imagined. I'd expected a man in his fifties, and he was closer to Mark's age—late thirties, early forties.

He was also shorter than I'd expected. He couldn't have been more than three inches taller than me. Coupled with his plain dark jeans and t-shirt and oversized, slightly nerdy glasses, he was the kind of man who wouldn't stand out in a crowd.

Even his walk had a certain practiced casualness to it that made me think he'd carefully curated his appearance so as not to be remembered. Smart for a private investigator. As much as I loved the old *Matlock* shows growing up, I'd always wondered why Conrad McMasters drove a flashy car.

Hal wouldn't make the same mistake of standing out.

The smile Hal gave me had a you-can-trust-me quality to it. He held out his hand. "Nice to finally meet you in person, Ms. Fitzhenry-Dawes."

I shook Hal's hand, but glanced at Anderson. "Does he still call you Mr. Taylor?"

Anderson flashed his toothpaste-commercial-white teeth. "No, but we've been working together since we both started our businesses."

I filed that tidbit away. Anderson hadn't founded his business immediately after law school. He'd worked at another firm first. So Hal must have had a career or worked somewhere else before he became a private investigator.

I matched Hal's smile. "I don't want to have to wait that long, so how about you call me Nicole now that we've met."

He ducked his head. "Yes, ma'am."

The ma'am came out almost second nature. Former military maybe?

"Do you mind if we use a conference room?" Anderson asked. "This was a weird case, and I have a half hour before my next meeting. I'd like to sit in."

I braced for the voice in my head that would tell me that the truth was Anderson didn't trust me.

It didn't come. For the first time, the self-critical voice stayed quiet. Instead, my head was filled only with my own thoughts. Anderson had mentioned from the start that he felt this case was interesting. Beyond that, it made sense for him to stay up-to-date on it. If the case didn't wrap up before I had the baby, Anderson might have to fill in for me for a little bit.

The guys hung back and let me pick a seat first. On his way by, Hal casually moved another chair closer to my feet.

He did it so nonchalantly that he might have been simply moving it out of the way. The fact that he didn't so much as glance in my direction, though, made me suspicious that he'd seen me with my feet propped up and was making sure I could do it again if need be.

They took seats across from me.

Hal pressed the Home button on his tablet and tapped the screen a couple of times. "I don't have any proof that the victim in the Williams case was a whistleblower, but I did find out a few things about the company she worked for that could support your client's story."

I held back a snort. Wouldn't that have been nice if Hal had found proof that Jordan was a whistleblower and that someone powerful in the company wanted her dead because of it?

Murder cases rarely handed another viable suspect on a platter that way, though.

Hal slid the tablet across the table to me. It was the first time I'd been acknowledged as the lead on the case. A warm feeling expanded inside my chest.

"Papyrus Medical had a new blood thinner that they'd been doing pre-marketing on for months," he said.

I glanced down at the screen. It was a picture of the type of promotional material that pharmaceutical reps left with doctors. I zoomed in. The informational overview said initial studies showed a 50 percent less chance of accidental bleeding than with conventional blood thinners like warfarin, and lab tests also showed a potential for reduced strain on the liver. The release date for the drug had already passed.

I slid his tablet back, then propped my feet up on the nearby chair. I might as well use it since it was there. "You're thinking Jordan had information on the drug?"

Hal handed the tablet over to Anderson, sitting on the other side of him, farther away from me. "They pulled the drug two weeks before release, saying they felt they needed to run more tests. Your victim might not have made anything public, but it sounds like she could have threatened to."

That made an even better motive for murdering her. Once she made what she knew public, the only reason for killing her would be revenge. If she hadn't gone public on the condition that they pull the drug, someone might have wanted to make it look like they were playing along until they could kill her. With her dead, they could easily release the drug in a few months, claiming their additional tests supported their earlier claims or showed even better results.

I sat quietly while Anderson looked at Hal's tablet.

He handed the tablet back to Hal. "That gives you a great start to creating reasonable doubt."

Sometimes Anderson sounded so much like my dad I'd have

sworn that he was my parents' child rather than me. For my parents and Anderson, all that mattered was winning. Creating enough reasonable doubt for an acquittal was a consolation prize for me. I wanted to prove that my client was innocent, and whenever I could, I wanted to find out the truth about what happened.

Despite how much better my feet felt when I had them propped up, I lowered them to the floor. If I wanted to be treated as an equal, even in my own business, I needed to make sure I acted the part.

"It's a start. To get more, I'll need to go to Jordan's office and speak with some of the people there. I'll start with her boss. I'd like to get a read on how much he or she knew."

Great, now I was putting *he or she* everywhere. Not knowing the gender of my baby was at least making my speech more grammatically correct. In the past, I would have said *what they knew* since English didn't have a singular generic pronoun the way other languages did.

Anderson's smile shifted. It was like watching ice crystals form over water. He softened his expression almost immediately. If I hadn't been looking at him at that exact moment, I would have missed it.

There could only be one reason that my statement would have made Anderson lose his professional mask, even for a second. "Not you, too."

Anderson's face relaxed, and his actor's smile disappeared

completely. "You and I work with evidence. If you looked at the evidence objectively, what conclusion would you draw?"

Likely the same one that he had, and that Mark had, and that Russ had. That my job placed me in danger. Still.

"You're the one who brought this client to me."

Anderson flattened his hands calmly on the table. "And I want you to take it. I also want you to take some extra precautions. If you're going to speak to anyone or investigate a location, take Hal with you."

Yeah, like that was going to work. Hal's firm—let alone Hal himself—was in high demand. He wasn't going to have time to follow me around, sometimes at a moment's notice.

Anderson shifted in his seat to face Hal.

Hal nodded. "We can make it work."

I sighed internally, but I didn't let it out. At least Hal was better than a bodyguard. Hal's background as a private investigator meant he'd know how to play the game. He wouldn't just stand around looking intimidating.

And if that's what it took to get everyone off my back about doing my job, I'd have to go along with it.

I pulled out my cell phone. "I'll call and try to get us an appointment with the company's CEO while you're here to check your calendar for availability as well."

Anderson pushed to his feet. "I'll leave you to it."

The paranoid voice that lived at the back of my brain said that I'd been played somehow. Anderson had certainly been interested in the case, but I couldn't shake the feeling that he'd also been there as a watchdog. Now that he'd passed that role over to Hal, he didn't need to stick around.

Hal read the number for the CEO's office off his tablet. He was certainly thorough in his research.

"Papyrus Medical. Martin Raymes' office," a woman's voice said.

Her tone made me think of a woman who wore large clip-on earrings that she had to remove every time the phone rang.

I mentally reviewed my schedule in my head. I didn't have anything this week that couldn't be moved, and I'd need to be flexible if I was going to bring Hal with me. He couldn't have many openings on short notice.

"I'd like to make an appointment to speak with Mr. Raymes."

She made an mm-hmm noise that sounded like she'd been trained to use it to reassure people that she was listening. "What's the meeting about?"

I'd been hoping she wouldn't ask. The last thing I wanted to do was tip anyone off that I suspected someone in their office had killed Jordan Williams. Or, more likely, put out a contract on her life. Her death had been so carefully staged that it would have taken someone with knowledge of the differences between suicidal hangings and execution hangings to pull it off. Most corporate executives, scientists, and pharmaceutical reps didn't have that sort of technical expertise.

That said, if I lied, she'd likely redirect me to another department. The company's CEO wouldn't take meetings that could be handled by someone else.

"Are you still there?" the woman asked.

"Yes." Even though it would give him advance warning, the truth seemed like the best tact to take. Or at least some of the truth. "I'm working the Jordan Williams case. I need to speak to Mr. Raymes about Papyrus Medical's competitors and whether any of them might have had reason to target Ms. Williams. Because of the sensitive nature of my questions, I can't speak to anyone else at the company. I'm sure you understand."

I made sure to add a note to my voice that said *I trust that you've dealt with enough sensitive information to see how important this is.*

If part of her job was to keep Martin Raymes' schedule clear of unnecessary appointments, then I needed to sound important.

"I understand. Of course." The sound of a mouse clicking on the other end of the line filled the quiet. "He has an opening at two o'clock on June 24th."

I sucked in a breath that left me feeling like I'd nearly swallowed my tongue. That was over a month away. We couldn't stall out the investigation that long. Zach's case would already be proceeding by then.

I smiled, hoping all the marketing advice that said people could hear it in your voice if you smiled was correct. "I'm sure if you told him what this is about, he'd find a spot for us sooner."

"He definitely would." A hint of defensiveness slid into her voice. "But he leaves tomorrow for China, and he won't return for a month."

6

*H*itting the disconnect button at the end of the call wasn't nearly as satisfying as slamming a classic phone back into the cradle would have been. It was more professional, though.

"No dice?" Hal asked.

I shook my head. I'd taken the June appointment anyway, just in case. "I'd still like to go to Papyrus Medical today and talk to some of Jordan's co-workers. I don't know how confidential my appointment and reason for coming will stay. If anyone there was involved, they'll want to cover it up."

Hal slid his tablet back into a black carrying case. "The risk of that seems low, doesn't it?"

On the surface, yes. I'd only told one person. But if living in Fair Haven had taught me anything, it was the speed of gossip.

"If she told the CEO or mentions to a friend at lunch that someone called asking questions about Jordan, it can spread."

Hal slung his bag over his shoulder. "If you go asking questions, it'll spread faster."

Hal's body language was relaxed. He didn't give me the impression that he was questioning my abilities or intelligence. His follow-up felt more like he was brainstorming with an equal.

A year ago, I wouldn't have been able to tell the difference.

"I'm not going to come at it directly. I can ask about changes in mood and imply Jordan's death is still being investigated as a suicide. Her co-workers might have noticed changes in her behavior, and if we're really lucky, I'll get an idea for who Jordan's friends were. There's a chance she confided in someone about what was going on."

The tick of the clock hands filled the room. There was something in Hal's expression that I couldn't quite read. Had he been trying to convince me not to go at all? There could only be two reasons for him to do that. Either he was too busy to work this case with me and he hadn't wanted to say so out of fear of losing all the work our firm gave his company. Or he was trying to earn favor with Anderson by keeping me out of potentially dangerous situations in the first place.

If it was the latter, we were in trouble. Going to a pharmaceutical company during the day when it was crowded with employees was the least dangerous thing I'd done on a case in a long time.

I'd give him the benefit of the doubt and assume it was the former. "I know you said you'd tag along with me on this case, but it's really not necessary. I'm sure you have other cases you need to work as well. I'll be fine going on my own."

Hal smiled. It made me think of a clown wiping off his makeup at the end of the performance. The character vanished, and for a second, the real man stood in front of me.

"I usually only get to see a part of any case I help with," Hal said. "It'll be a nice change to see it from this side. Variety prevents burnout, after all."

Making me feel like I was doing him a favor was a classic switch technique. His demeanor had enough honesty in it that I couldn't call him on anything specific, but I still couldn't help the feeling that I was also somehow being played. That seemed to be happening a lot of late.

But if it let me pursue this case, I'd play along. For now.

The guard at the door of Papyrus Medical flipped over the top page on his clipboard and his gaze ran down the second page.

Hal shot me a what-are-you-hoping-to-accomplish look. Our names weren't going to be on the list because we didn't have an appointment.

That might or might not matter. I'd been raised by parents

who believed that a roadblock was an opportunity to either find a creative way around it or call in a favor and have it moved.

The guard looked up from his list. "I'm sorry, ma'am. You're not on the list, and I can't let you in without approval. Who was your appointment with?"

And there was the flaw in my hasty plan. I only knew the name of one person at Papyrus Medical. "Martin Raymes. And if we miss this appointment, we'll have to wait until June when he's back from his trip."

The guard glanced at his paperwork and then back behind him where people going in and out passed through security checkpoints.

I'd thrown enough truth into my lie to make him uncertain.

He slowly shook his head, almost like his mind and his body still weren't in agreement on the right thing to do. "I can't let you in unless you're on the list. Do you want me to call Mr. Raymes' office?"

No. I definitely *didn't* want him doing that. We'd end up escorted to our car. "That's okay." I pulled my cell phone out of my purse and inclined my head toward the front door. "We'll step out, and I'll make the call myself. I'm sure we can sort this out."

Hal held the door open for me. He showed professionalism by not saying *I told you so*. I might have said something if I hadn't been the one who foolishly thought I could talk my way past the guards.

We stopped out of sight of the guards inside. I'd claimed I planned to call Mr. Raymes' office. The guards didn't need to see that I wasn't doing that. If they got suspicious enough, they could call the police and have us removed from the property.

Hal stood with his hands clasped behind his back and his feet slightly apart. He said nothing.

He was taking this observer status to the extreme. Normally when someone else tagged along on my cases, they contributed. Memories of Mark joining me flittered across my mind, and a little pang hit my chest.

But I couldn't expect Mark to always be my sidekick. He had his own job to do.

At least this time I could discuss the case with him. He hadn't worked this case, and Zach signed a waiver allowing me to consult with whatever experts I needed to.

Hal's continued silence made me want to break out into the chicken dance just to see if he'd react. I felt the same way around those street artists who pretended to be statues and the guards I'd seen at Buckingham Palace when Uncle Stan took me with him to London for a medical conference.

Hal didn't even ask what I planned to do next.

So this was all in my court. If we were going to get into Papyrus Medical before my appointment with Martin Raymes next month, I'd have to come up with the idea for how to do it.

I looked up at the building.

The metal and glass glinted in the sun.

I blinked and shaded my eyes. The building had to be twenty stories high. According to the signs out front, the pharmaceutical company was the only business in the building. That meant a high number of employees and an HR department. If I could get in touch with someone there, we might have another way in. Someone needed to clean the personal items out of Jordan's desk, after all. When I'd asked Zach more questions about Jordan's job, he'd mentioned he'd never been to Jordan's place of work, which meant he hadn't collected them himself.

I glanced at Hal's bag. He still carried it over his shoulder despite my suggestion that he leave it in the car. "Do you have the number for human resources here?"

He raised his eyebrows as if to say *Do I look like an amateur?* He pulled out his tablet and read the number for me while I dialed.

A woman answered, introducing herself as Lisa.

"Hi, umm, I'm hoping I got the right department."

I made sure to make my voice sound small and uncertain, with a bit of a shake.

Hal stopped with his tablet halfway back into his case. He slid it in more slowly, as if he didn't want to miss my performance. I must have surprised him.

Yup, that fumble with the guards at the door wasn't my best work. Mark could have vouched for that if he'd been here. When we'd first met, I'd been so convincing when working a source that he'd thought I was flirting.

"If you haven't," the woman on the other end of the line said, "I'd be happy to redirect you."

There wasn't even a hint of annoyance or rush in her tone. Probably patience was a quality required from anyone working in HR. Either that, or she was a genuinely nice person. Unfortunately for her, the nice people were often the easiest to play.

"I came to collect the belongings of a family member who passed away, but the guards at the door said I couldn't come in without an appointment. How do I go about getting one of those?"

"Jordan." The woman's voice took on that soft sound that people got when they didn't know someone who'd died personally, but they still wanted to be respectful of what had happened. "I've called her brother a couple of times. Jordan's replacement starts on Monday, so we can't leave her desk untouched anymore." A pause. "And you are?"

As if she'd just realized I hadn't said how I was related to Jordan. They couldn't give her stuff away to just anyone. It had to be the next of kin.

"That's why we're here." I snuck a peek at Hal. To pull this off, he was going to have to play along rather than just follow me around like some sort of mute guard dog. As a private investigator, he should be able to play a part. It was one of the reasons I'd agreed to having him join me. He'd likely just been waiting for instructions from me. "Zach didn't feel up to collecting Jordan's things alone, so he waited for a time when we could both get a day off work. I don't know when we'll be able to manage that again. Is there any way we can get an appointment with someone today who'll be able to see us?"

The sound of a desk chair rolling across the floor filled the pause. "I have a half hour free now. You said you're here?"

I confirmed that we were out in the parking lot, and she said she'd meet us at the front door.

Hal cast a sidelong glance in my direction. "That was both impressive and frightening."

I grinned at him. "So people tell me." I motioned to his bag. "You might want to put that in the car now. I doubt Zach would bring a tablet and case notes to clear out his sister's desk. We don't need to draw any more attention to ourselves on the way in or out."

We dropped his bag in the car—tucking it under the seat in the back so he felt a bit more secure about leaving it behind—and went back to the front door. A woman in a charcoal-gray pantsuit with a coral-colored blouse waited outside the front doors. She had her phone out.

She must have caught sight of us approaching because she tucked her phone back into her pocket. She headed straight for Hal with her hand out. "You must be Zach. I wanted to say how sorry all of us are for your loss. Jordan was a valuable member of the team here. She'll be missed."

Hal accepted her handshake. "Thank you. It's been a hard time."

Lisa was nodding. She turned in my direction as if waiting for an introduction. I'd hoped she'd forgotten that I hadn't actually given my name on the phone, but apparently, being in HR, she was good at remembering names—and when someone had conveniently skipped giving one.

Hal held a hand out sideways in my direction, and I moved in closer. "This is my wife, Nikki. She's the one who called you."

I cringed inside. Mark would definitely not like me pretending to be someone else's wife, but Hal had made the right call. Lisa would have noticed my wedding ring at some point, and we couldn't pretend I was Zach and Jordan's sister. They didn't have one. Lisa or someone else we might run into could know that.

I wrapped a hand around my barely-there baby bump—hopefully adding some credence to Hal's story—and shook Lisa's hand as well.

"I can't get you around the security," she said, "but I'll try to get us through the process as quickly as possible."

She led us through the doors. There was only one line in and one line out. That meant we were going to have to pass by the guard we'd spoken to before. Our story had changed since then. If he brought up our supposed meeting with Martin Raymes, Lisa would know we'd lied to her.

Lisa flashed the guard her badge. "They're not on the list, but it's okay."

I had to head off any questions from him about why we were now with someone from HR.

When the truth would hurt you, my dad always said, *direct the attention somewhere else.*

It was basically the lawyer version of a magician's trick. The best way to keep from having to admit to a damaging truth was to make sure no one ever asked about it.

I plunked my purse down on the silver table. "This seems like a lot of security for a company that produces medications. Are you worried about people stealing them and selling them on the streets?"

Lisa put her cell phone into the little basket provided and stepped through the metal detector or whatever the machine was. "It's more about protecting our trade secrets and patents." She picked her cell phone back up on the other side. She tilted her head toward the security line people were waiting in to exit. "We don't want people walking in off the street and seeing what we're developing, and our employees aren't allowed to take anything home with them. Even our email programs are all internal."

All the security protocols would have made it difficult for Jordan to get any evidence of wrongdoing out. She must have taken some major risks to make sure the company didn't get away with whatever they were doing.

I stepped forward, toward the metal detector. A hand landed on my shoulder, stopping me.

7

*M*y breath clogged in my throat like it'd turned solid. Busted.

My brain tripped over itself, trying to figure out an excuse that would still get us into the building. Nothing came to mind.

I eased around to face behind me. Only Hal stood there. The guard was still poking through my purse.

Hal nodded down at my belly. "I don't know if these things are safe for babies."

Crap. If x-rays could hurt babies, x-ray machines might be able to as well. I hadn't even thought about that. Shouldn't I have thought about it? I'd been so caught up in the investigation that I'd almost put my baby in danger without even realizing it.

What kind of a mom was I going to be if work distracted me so much that I didn't take proper care of my baby? That was what Russ had been saying, after all. All his dramatics aside, he'd been insisting that I needed to think about protecting myself, and by extension, my baby.

Hal removed his hand from my shoulder. "Is this safe for pregnant woman?" he asked loudly enough for the guard to hear him.

The guard zipped up my purse and put it on the conveyor belt that took it to the other side of the machine. "Yeah. It's a metal detector, not an x-ray machine like in the hospitals. It only uses the same type of radiation that your household appliances do."

He watched me closely enough that I got the impression he suspected us of something. At the very least, he suspected I wanted to bring something into the building that I shouldn't. He'd taken extra time searching my purse. He might even think I was faking being pregnant to have an excuse for not walking through the metal detector.

Since it was safe for the baby and I wasn't trying to sneak anything in, I had no reason not to.

I walked through. No alarms went off. I'd put everything that could set it off into my purse, just like at the airport.

Hal came through after me. We collected our belongings and followed Lisa to the elevators. The whole building had a clean, almost sterile feel to it, even the elevators. Their sides were shiny reflective metal. It almost felt like they were leaving a subconscious message for their employees that there was no place to hide here. Everything they did reflected back and would be seen.

We stopped at the tenth floor. I'd expected to come out into a hallway, but the elevator doors slid back to reveal an open room that seemed to take up the whole floor. Rows of cubicles filled the space, but their walls were so low that I could see the screens of all the computers.

"Jordan's desk was this way," Lisa said.

She took us to the far back corner.

Jordan's desk was one of the corner spots. The cubicle was technically set up so that her computer screen should have faced out into the room, placing Jordan's back to everyone. Jordan had managed to maneuver her monitor so that it didn't directly face the rest of the room. A person had to be standing to the only open side of her cubicle to see her screen. It would have required her to torque her body at an angle to work, but she would have had privacy that no one else did.

I could think of only one reason for someone to do that. Zach had been telling the truth. Before she died, Jordan had been working on something that she didn't want anyone else to see.

I couldn't prove yet that it'd gotten her killed, but it seemed like we were looking in the right direction.

We needed to get a look at what was on Jordan's computer. That meant getting rid of Lisa for a few minutes. And hoping the computer either didn't have a password—which was possible in a company where the powers that be didn't want their employees to be able to keep secrets—or that Hal had some trick to hack into the computer if it did have a password.

I snapped my fingers and shot Hal a look that said *We screwed up.* "We didn't bring a box. I knew we were forgetting something." I gave Lisa a sheepish smile. "I don't suppose there's a box that we could use?"

"Umm…" Lisa glanced back over her shoulder. "Sure. There's probably one in the mail room or stock." She waved to a man heading to a nearby cubicle, his arms full of files. "This is Jordan's family. They're here to collect up her things. Could you find them a box they could use?"

He mumbled condolences at us, dropped off his files, and headed back the way he'd come. The way he practically scurried away made him seem happy to be able to run an errand rather than stick around Jordan's presumably grief-stricken relatives. Some people didn't know how to deal with others' grief.

Bad news for my plan: Lisa was sticking around.

Thinking about it more, Lisa probably couldn't leave us alone. A company who took their security this seriously likely had rules in place for visitors. Leaving us unaccompanied for any length of time might cost her job. I didn't want to do that to her, especially considering how nice she'd been to us.

Hal pulled open one of the desk drawers. "Should we take everything?"

To Lisa, it would sound like he was a normal grieving brother, unsure of how much to keep. It was a challenge every family faced when they lost someone. Did you keep even mundane items out of sentimentality, or did you select a few valuable things and get rid of the rest?

To me, the question had a different meaning. Did we only take things that might logically be connected to our case? The problem was, we didn't know what might be connected. And if Jordan had been smuggling information out of the company, she'd have had to be sneaky about it. We might not find her method if we only took the obvious items.

"Take everything. We can sort through it at home when we have more time."

We couldn't pack up anything until the other employee came back with a box, though. Maybe, while we waited, I could distract Lisa enough that Hal could crack Jordan's computer.

I needed to get Lisa to turn her back to Hal. Most people would turn to face someone who was speaking to them, so if I moved and struck up a conversation, she should follow along with me.

I rubbed the small of my back. "This baby eats up all my energy. Is it alright if I sit down?"

I slid around her and sank into the chair belonging to the man she'd sent on a hunt for a box. It was a bit presumptuous on my part, but we might not have long until he returned. Besides, what kind of a person was really going to tell a pregnant lady she couldn't sit down?

My next challenge would be to get Lisa talking about something that would hold her attention. "I didn't realize Jordan worked for such a big company." I stretched a hand out and waved it in the direction of the other cubicles—the ones away from Jordan's cubicle and Hal. Hal rolled closer to Jordan's computer and took out his phone. I made eye contact with Lisa, adding another layer of security that she'd stay focused on me. "What type of responsibilities does the HR department have in a place like this?"

Lisa's answer was short, but I levied a string of follow-up questions at her.

Halfway through telling me about all the steps in their hiring process, she stopped. Her gaze shifted up over my left shoulder. She made a *come here* gesture. The sharp tap of woman's heels approached from behind me. Hal shoved his phone into his pocket and spun around, away from Jordan's computer.

"Andrea," Lisa said, "I thought you might want to say hello. This is Jordan's brother Zach and his wife."

Hopefully Hal had enough time with Jordan's computer. We wouldn't likely get another chance.

I stood and shifted to face the woman behind me.

She wore a long white lab coat over a pale grey A-line dress. Despite being swathed in a lab coat, her form was all angles.

Even without heels, she would have been inches taller than I was. I had to tilt my head back to meet her gaze.

Except she wasn't looking at me. She was looking at Hal.

With narrowed eyes.

"I don't know what these people told you," she said, "but that's not Jordan's brother."

a cold shiver ran straight down my core, like I'd swallowed an ice cube whole.

With one sentence, we'd likely lost any chance of figuring out if Jordan got killed because of something going on here. Worse, they might think we were sent here by a competitor to spy on them. They could try to have us arrested for industrial espionage. My baby would spend time in jail before he or she was ever born.

Breathe, Nicole, I told myself.

Psychologists say humans have one of two reactions in situations of stress or danger—fight or flight. My instincts wanted to send me into flight. My parents would say there was a third option—lie.

We could pretend like we didn't know what she was talking about. We could hold to our story. If Andrea had only briefly seen a picture, we still had a chance of convincing her she was wrong.

That seemed to be the path Hal had chosen. His eyebrows had drawn down as if she'd come in and said he was an elephant.

Hal looked in my direction, obviously expecting me to play along. I raised my shoulders in an *I don't know what's she's talking about, either* gesture.

I redirected my gaze to Andrea. "Who are you?"

Her body stiffened, her shoulders straight back. She turned so that she faced me full-on—toes, hips, shoulders, and eyes all pointing directly at me.

Crap. It wasn't something as simple as she'd seen a picture. We were busted. She *knew*.

"I'm Jordan's friend." Her tone was like a punch, but one that pulled up at the last second like it hit a wall of grief before it could make contact with me. "She set me up on a blind date with her brother less than a year ago. I don't know who that is"—she pointed a stiff finger at Hal—"but I know it isn't Jordan's brother. The game you're playing won't work on me."

I'd hoped that we would meet someone who'd been close to Jordan. I hadn't thought we'd run into someone who'd also know what Zach looked like. Then again, I hadn't originally intended for us to pose as Zach and his fictitious wife at all.

Lisa backed a step away from me. She grabbed the phone from the desk beside her. "I'm calling security."

Hal glanced at me, but stayed quiet. He wasn't the team leader in this mission. I was.

I held up both my hands toward Lisa in a *wait* sign. "Give us a chance to explain. Please."

Lisa shook her head, the phone still to her ear. "So you can tell me another lie about who you are and why you're here. I could already lose my job over this. For all I know, management is going to think I was in on whatever you came here to do."

The hand not holding the phone tapped against her thigh, like she was urging security to answer.

This place really did take security and informational privacy seriously if Lisa was that terrified of losing her job. If they'd fire her for being tricked into letting us into the secure building, it spoke to the lengths they might have gone to had they thought Jordan planned to expose them.

But I wouldn't be able to prove it if they kicked us out now.

Lisa cared about her job. Andrea cared about Jordan. If I could get through to her, she might have a better chance of stopping Lisa from turning us in than I would.

"My real name is Nicole Fitzhenry-Dawes. I'm a criminal defense attorney, and I've been hired by Jordan's brother to defend him for Jordan's murder." I held my purse out to Andrea. "You can check for yourself that I'm telling the truth. Look at my driver's license and my business card."

Andrea crossed her arms. "I heard that the police think Zach killed her."

Heard it and—it seemed—believed they were right. I lowered my purse. Not a glowing endorsement for Zach since Andrea had actually met him. "I don't think Zach did it. We think she was killed because she was trying to expose something that was happening here. With the drug that was recently pulled right before its release. The blood thinner."

Behind me, Lisa said, "Hold for a minute, please."

Andrea looked over my head. Presumably she met Lisa's gaze and they were having some sort of silent conversation with their eyes.

"We came here to find evidence," I said softly. "To get justice for Jordan."

"I'll call you back if we still need you," Lisa said.

I thought I heard the click of her setting the handset back into its cradle, but I wasn't about to look around to find out. If they were considering helping us, then any sudden movement on my part could break that channel of thought.

Andrea ran her hands down the sides of her lab coat. She looked behind me one more time. "Jordan did find something. But it's not what you think."

9

*L*isa moved past me, touching my shoulder on her way by. "We should take this to my office."

Andrea followed behind her. I trailed after them both, and I felt more than saw Hal take up position on my heels. I had to admit—he was a good wingman. I didn't have to give him cues or signals for how to act, and he didn't panic the way one of my friends might when I put them into...interesting situations.

The man Lisa had sent to find a box met us halfway across the room.

He held it out to her. "Found one. It wasn't easy."

"We don't need it anymore," she said.

The man's expression flickered between *You've got to be kidding me* and *Can I call it road rage if I'm not in a car?*

I gave him my best appreciative smile on our way past. "Thank you, anyway."

He stood holding the box as if he wasn't sure what to do with it now. On the upside, if Zach did suddenly decide to collect Jordan's pens and coffee mug, he'd have a way to pack it up.

Neither Lisa nor Andrea said anything as we filed back into the elevator. My heart felt like it was rising higher into my throat with every floor we went up. If Hal hadn't been with me, my mind might have started to play tricks on me, thinking they were going to dispose of me the way someone had of Jordan.

Thankfully, it'd be much harder to get rid of two of us.

Lisa's office, it turned out, had actual walls. They were glass walls so they didn't add any more visual privacy—status quo in this place—but they'd block sound at least. That was probably a requirement for an HR office. It would have violated privacy had people not been able to speak to someone in HR without risking anyone who walked by overhearing.

The room only had three chairs. Hal pulled one out for me and then moved back. He stood in the corner nearest my chair, leaning back against the wall.

Lisa sank into the chair behind the desk, and Andrea pulled the remaining chair around to the side so that she was sitting at the short end of the desk rather than sharing either side with one of us.

It was interesting positioning, almost like she saw herself as the bridge between the two of us.

Lisa shot her a look that seemed to say *Are we doing the right thing?*

Andrea's shoulders bunched up in response—a version of *What choice do we have?*

Lisa shifted in a way that made me think she'd crossed her legs. "This information isn't public knowledge. How do we know that you're not reporters posing as Zach Williams' lawyers?"

I jutted my chin toward her computer. "Search for my name."

She swiveled her chair toward the screen and placed her hands on her keyboard.

I knew what she'd find. Anderson had hired a PR company to make sure our website was search-engine optimized. It came up as the first result when anyone put in either of our names or a bevy of other search terms. My bio page on our website included a picture. She'd be able to tell at a glance that I was who I said I was. I'd balked at the picture when Anderson wanted me to sit for professional headshots. Now I was thankful. Otherwise, she might have worried I was using Nicole Fitzhenry-Dawes' name. Even my driver's license might not have convinced her since that could have been forged.

Lisa shifted until her chair faced me again. She gave a tiny nod in Andrea's direction. "I'll let Andrea tell the story. I was only brought in at the end because of the personnel issues the situation created."

I scooted toward the edge of my seat. Assuming Lisa didn't

mean she'd been dispatched to kill Jordan herself, "personnel issues" sounded like someone had been fired.

Andrea's jaw tightened in a way that made her face look even more angular than it had before. "If you're looking for someone else to pin Jordan's death on, you won't find it here."

Not a flattering assessment of what criminal lawyers did, but not entirely inaccurate, either. My parents would definitely be working this angle as a way to cast reasonable doubt on their client's guilt. I might use the same information to do that, but only because I thought my client was innocent.

Defending myself, though, wouldn't do any good.

I folded my hands in my lap and waited. If Andrea needed to rail, she could rail, as long as in the end she told me what she knew.

"I understand," I said. "Right now, we're just sorting through leads and looking for the truth."

She leaned forward, and her chair squeaked. "Jordan was sort of a mediator between departments. She worked with lab techs like me and helped the marketing department and sales reps understand the product well enough that they could answer whatever questions came up. She's good at that because she's naturally skeptical. She had a knack for anticipating questions."

Andrea didn't seem to notice that she'd spoken about Jordan in the present tense. I'd once heard a TED Talk where the speaker talked about how we often *moved forward* but we didn't always *move on* from the death of someone we cared about. It was why it was so easy to slip into talking about a dead loved one in the present tense. They might be gone, but for us, they were still present in some sense. It'd stuck with me because it was how I felt about my Uncle Stan. Even though he was gone, his influence on my life kept going. I wouldn't be married to Mark if Uncle Stan hadn't been brave enough to leave a career he no longer loved.

Andrea tightened her lab coat around her. "The claims around our newest drug seemed too good to be true to her, even though they came with the clinical trial results to prove their effectiveness. Jordan had experience with blood thinners thanks to her dad's strokes. She started to dig."

She glanced at Lisa. Neither of them wanted to be the one to go too far, tell too much, and end up fired.

Lisa nodded again.

"Jordan went so far as to speak to some of the patients in the trial and with their family doctors. She found out the results of the tests were falsified."

That much I'd guessed, and Andrea had confirmed when she said that Jordan had found something. But she'd also said it wasn't what we thought. Right now, it sounded like exactly what we thought.

It sounded like Jordan caught the company trying to lie to the public.

It took all my willpower not to glance back at Hal and give away what I was thinking.

Andrea had gone quiet. Her throat moved like she was swallowing hard, battling memories of Jordan.

"What happened after that?" I asked quietly.

"Sorry." Andrea straightened slightly in her chair. "She brought her suspicions to me. She wanted me to look over the documentation as a fresh set of eyes, in case she'd missed something that could explain the discrepancy." Andrea's lips narrowed. "She hadn't."

I peeked at Lisa. She was watching Andrea and nodding along in that subconscious way that people had when they agreed with what they were hearing on a deep level. So at least as far as Lisa knew, what Andrea was saying was the truth.

Andrea had been holding her lab coat closed as if it were protective gear. She let it fall open and planted her hands on her knees. "I know you're thinking that someone here killed Jordan to keep her quiet, but that's how I know you're wrong. Jordan and I went together to talk to the CEO. He made the call to stop production on the drug immediately and to hold all orders while we were in the office with him."

All that meant was that he hadn't wanted them to realize he was in on it. It didn't mean he hadn't killed Jordan to keep her quiet. And, if I was right, that meant Andrea could be next on his hit list. "He might have done that so you wouldn't suspect the company already knew about the falsified studies."

Andrea's upper lip moved enough that I guessed it was as close to a smile as she was going to get under the circumstances. "Jordan didn't just come to me because we were friends. She came to me because my uncle's the CEO. And he's a lot of things, but a good liar isn't one of them. When my family plays Werewolf at the holidays, he always has to be the moderator because no one wants to end up as a werewolf with him."

I'd never played Werewolf, but I'd heard of it. Players were secretly dealt cards that told them they were either werewolves or villagers. The villagers were supposed to figure out who the werewolves were, and the goal for werewolves was to not be caught. It was called a social deduction game. It might as well have been called a find-out-who-in-your-family-is-the-best-bluffer game.

If Andrea was telling me the truth, it also meant that Jordan wasn't a whistleblower after all. She was a conscientious employee who told an honest company about something shady happening within their walls. And the company dealt with it.

That situation was probably less rare than a whistleblower situation. It was simply less publicized because most companies wanted to keep internal corruption quiet. While some brands believed that any press was good press, that wasn't the case when you were in a business where you needed consumers to trust you.

"Did you find out who was behind it?" Hal asked.

"It was the chemist who'd designed the drug," Lisa said. "He was fired, as you might imagine. The regulatory body is also taking action, and it'll be years before he can hope to work in this field again."

If anyone would hire him after this. More likely, this meant the end of his career.

Lisa and Andrea might not read into Hal's question, but I knew what he was really trying to find out—was there now someone out there who held a grudge against Jordan?

"Did the employee who was fired know Jordan was the one who outed him?" I asked.

Lisa nodded. "As a company, we're guilty for not independently verifying his results, but we didn't want to compound that mistake by potentially falsely accusing an innocent person. When Jordan and Andrea brought this to the company's attention, we weren't sure who was behind it. The investigation went on for months, and both Jordan and Andrea were a part of all of it."

The back of my neck prickled in that spiders-with-icy-feet kind of way. That meant that if the fired employee held enough of a grudge to kill Jordan, Andrea might be next.

And no one was looking at him as a suspect. Papyrus Medical had kept it so quiet that the police might not even have realized there was a potential suspect through her work.

I leaned forward toward Andrea in what I hoped was an *I'm concerned for you* way rather than a *vulture circling* kind of way. Human body language wasn't an exact science. So much of

it came down to context and interpretation. I didn't want Andrea
to shut down because she misinterpreted.

"Have you received any threatening calls or letters?" I asked.
"If there's even a possibility that Jordan was killed because of
this, you could be in danger, too."

Andrea's gaze shifted to the side like she was thinking. She
shook her head. "Dexter was angry, but his anger seemed to be
general, not specific. He said he did it because he knew further
trials would prove his claims about the drug, and he didn't want
patients to have to wait any longer for a medication that was
better than what they'd been taking."

It was like I'd been given puzzle pieces that belonged to two
different puzzles. Jordan's murder was methodical and targeted.
Whoever had done it had planned carefully to kill her. They'd
have had plenty of time for second thoughts.

That person and the picture Andrea painted of Dexter the
chemist didn't have the perfect overlap I might wish for.

Dexter sounded like he had a savior complex. A savior
complex often created angels-of-mercy killers who euthanized
patients who were suffering. It didn't tend to result in someone
who killed a perfectly healthy person out of anger.

Not even if that person was in the way of the mercy killer
"helping" the people they saw as needing them. Killing a healthy
bystander—whatever the reason—wouldn't fit with the fictional
reality the angel-of-mercy killers lived in. As soon as they took a

life where the killing wasn't to "save" someone, it would fracture their identity.

General anger didn't fit, either. General anger was the kind of anger that resulted in disgruntled employees bringing a gun to work and shooting everyone they worked with. It was also the kind of anger that led to nothing more than the former employee grumbling about how unfairly the company treated them. It wasn't the kind of anger that singled out one person to target.

All that said, if Dexter was smart enough to orchestrate fake medical study results, he was also smart enough to come up with a story for why he'd done it that might have gotten him off. The company could have taken pity on him and given him a second chance rather than firing him.

He might have falsified the study results for another reason.

Lisa glanced at the clock on the wall. "My next appointment is in five minutes."

If I could only ask one or two more questions, I had to choose them strategically. "Did you believe the reasons Dexter gave for falsifying the results?"

Lisa twitched in her seat like she hadn't noticed when Andrea gave Dexter's name before. It was likely that neither of them was supposed to divulge as much as they'd told us already, let alone who the fired employee was.

Andrea had been shaking her head almost before I finished asking my question. "We get perks if we're on a team that designs a new drug that goes to market. It's how the company incentivizes creativity and hard work. Dexter wasn't the kind of guy to even hold the elevator for you. I heard him on the phone at lunch once arguing with his wife about something she'd bought, and then trying to convince the credit card company afterward that the charge was fraudulent." She looked over at Lisa as if expecting her to corroborate the next part. "I told the advisory board at the time that I didn't believe his story about trying to rush the drug to market for altruistic reasons."

"I remember that," Lisa said. "It ended up being what swung the board's decision. If Dex—if the former employee were going to go after anyone, it'd have been you, not Jordan."

Or, more likely, he would have gone after both of them.

This wasn't just about figuring out who killed Jordan Williams anymore. It was about making sure that Andrea didn't end up dead as well.

inding out whether someone might be a killer or not only got harder when you didn't know the person's last name. Dexter wasn't a common name, but even Hal couldn't come up with contact information for someone with nothing more to go on than their first name.

I pulled my phone out of my purse. "Do you have current contact information for the employee who was involved in this?"

"I think we've given all the help we can offer." Lisa pushed back her chair and stood in that way that people had when they wanted to get you out of their office or house without being rude. "My next appointment is probably here already."

She couldn't have given a clearer *no* if she'd actually said it. They weren't supposed to tell us the first name of the man involved—they probably weren't technically supposed to tell us anything at all—and she certainly wasn't going to risk her job by giving me his last name or his phone number.

I knew what Hal's next job would be. We'd have to figure out who the employee was, whether he'd had any contact with Jordan afterward, and if he had an alibi for her time of death.

Lisa moved around her desk and shook my hand. She inclined her head toward Hal. "Is he really your husband at least?"

When I told this story later to Mark, I might omit this part. Now that we were married, his jealous streak had gone into hibernation. I didn't want to wake it up. "He's my firm's private investigator."

Lisa widened her eyes. "Being a lawyer must be big business if you can afford to have a PI tag along after you half the day. I tried to hire one to get me proof that my cheating ex-husband was doing exactly what I suspected he was doing, and I practically had to take a second job to pay for it."

I gave her a smile, but it felt like I'd cut it out of a magazine. Private investigators who spied on cheating spouses tended to be able to charge whatever they wanted if they also came with a decent reputation. People would pay whatever it took to either get their divorce or set their mind at ease.

Still, Hal's firm was the most highly-respected in Michigan. Anderson only worked with the best. And Hal was the boss.

Tagging along after me all day wasn't a smart business move. He couldn't have so few cases on his plate that he was bored and looking for entertainment. While we respected each other as professionals, we hadn't met before today. We weren't friends. He had no emotional stake in my well-being.

Anderson sitting in on our meeting this morning seemed less in-the-moment and much more strategic the longer I thought about it.

I shook Andrea's hand, and we headed down the hallway, but it was like the actions were a TV show playing in the background.

There was only one reason I could think of that he'd given up all this time to shadow me and keep me safe. Someone had paid him to do it.

I could ask him who'd done it, but Hal was a professional. A professional trained to lie and with the obligation to protect the identity of his clients. All he'd likely tell me was that he couldn't tell me.

I'd have to sniff out the source for myself and deal with it. As much as I appreciated Hal's help today, whoever had hired him couldn't keep spending large sums of money to have him trail after me wherever I went like some sort of guard dog.

We entered the elevator. Hal pressed the button for the ground floor, and the door started to slide shut. An arm jutted into the crack, and the doors popped back open.

Andrea stepped inside. "I'm going down too."

She pressed the button for a floor midway between where

we were now and the lobby. The doors slid shut completely this time.

She moved back a step so that she stood with one of her shoulder nearly touching mine. The air in my lungs felt like it turned solid. She was too close. Like she wanted me to know that she was bigger than me and stronger than me and, if Hal hadn't been here, I would have been at her mercy.

You can't control the triggers, my counsellor's voice played in my head. *You can only control your reaction. Ground yourself. Box breathe.*

After my last case where I'd ended up buried alive, it seemed like I couldn't help jumping to paranoid conclusions. I was trying to work through it with my counsellor and in my PTSD support group, but it was a slower process this time. All the dangerous situations I'd ended up in were like a compounding injury, where every time I reinjured myself, the recovery time was longer.

In that way, Russ had a point. Not that I was going to admit it to him. Especially not since he topped my list of people who might have hired Hal.

"Pen and paper," Andrea said.

She said it quick and low, and for the first time, I wondered if there were cameras in the elevator. That would explain her strange positioning. She was using her body to block the camera so that it wouldn't be able to see us exchange a note.

I hadn't even thought about the possibility of cameras in here, maybe even recording microphones. If there were, it was a good thing Hal and I hadn't gotten into the elevator alone. We likely would have started discussing the case.

I scrambled around in my purse. All I could find for paper was a coffee receipt. I handed it to her along with a pen.

She scribbled something and shoved it back at me. I tucked it into my purse without even looking at it.

The elevator jolted to a stop, the doors opened, and Andrea stepped out without another word.

If my suspicions were correct, we needed to wait to look at the note or discuss anything more until we were out of this building. This place had less privacy than a jail.

ANDREA'S NOTE WAS ONLY TWO WORDS LONG.

Dexter Ruffalo.

The way we'd gotten his full name wasn't ideal, but it did tell me I'd been right about who cared more about Jordan's murder investigation. Lisa's loyalty was to the company. Andrea's, as I'd suspected, was to Jordan. It meant she might be willing to sneak me other information if we needed it.

Hal only waited long enough for me to buckle in before he pulled out of the parking space. "Do you think they were telling the truth?"

Some people would only ask a question like that if they

thought they'd been lied to but didn't want to come right out and say it. Hal's training more closely resembled mine, though.

In our line of work, we asked questions rather than making statements because we didn't want to bias any opinions. The more people who arrived at a conclusion independently, the more likely we were to come to the correct conclusion. At least, that's what my parents had taught me.

So did I think they told us the truth?

When they were telling their story, Lisa and Andrea had both come across to me as genuine. Their body language hadn't suggested that my questions about Jordan and the new drug made them uncomfortable. The company didn't want what had gone on getting out to the press—for obvious reasons—but it sounded like the company had been grateful to Jordan. She'd saved them. Had someone discovered the new drug wasn't all they claimed it to be once the drug had already gone to market, the fallout could have destroyed the company completely.

Hal glanced over at me expectantly.

"I do think they were telling the truth," I said. "At least as they know it."

"Agreed. What's your next step? If we'll be doing other in-person interviews, I want to block enough time in my schedule."

Until I knew who was paying Hal for accompanying me and talk to them about it, I didn't want to eat up more of their money. For now, we'd get Hal back on the firm's payroll, doing research.

I passed Hal the slip of paper. "We need to know as much about Dexter Ruffalo and what he's been doing since he was fired as possible."

He tucked it into his pocket. "I'll dig up what I can find."

And, in the meantime, I'd try to figure out who hired me a bodyguard behind my back.

11

Mandy's car was pulling out of the Sugarwood driveway as I pulled in. At least I wouldn't have to walk the dogs if Mandy had been there, and it was Mark's night to cook. No one had warned me prior to pregnancy how much faster I'd get tired. When I'd mentioned it to my mom on the phone last week, her response had been *Of course you're exhausted. A baby is essentially a parasite, Nicole.*

Only my mother could refer to her unborn grandchild as a parasite and have it not sound like she hated babies. Coming from her, it sounded like a strangely practical medical diagnosis. Anything that lived in the body of another organism and obtained the fuel it needed to survive from that host body was, technically, a parasite.

I dropped my purse, keys, and jacket inside the front door,

and Toby and Velma swarmed me with full body wags. The aroma of grilling beef filled the house, and my mouth watered.

No one had warned me I'd be extra-hungry when I wasn't sick to my stomach, either.

Mark smiled at me from beside the stove. "I got home late, so it was either burgers or takeout. I made sure we had lettuce, tomatoes, and provolone."

I used both hands to pet the dogs so neither one of them got jealous. "Are you trying to buy my vote about whether we find out the baby's gender using my favorite cheese?"

He smiled in the way that made his dimples pop out. "Maybe. Will it work?"

I unsuccessfully tried to hold back a return smile and shook my head. It was turning into a game between us. Who could convince the other to change their mind? So far, we were still at a stalemate. My next gambit was to show Mark the cute toys we could buy for the baby's room once we knew if we were having a boy or a girl.

Mark set aside the spatula and met me halfway across the room. He leaned in for a kiss, and Velma shoved her body between us. She used her weight to force Mark back a step.

He sighed. "I knew it'd be harder to get time with you once the baby was born. I didn't realize it'd happen sooner than that thanks to our dog."

"At least she's not growling at you."

Both dogs' behavior had shifted since my pregnancy. It

seemed like the natural tendencies inside them intensified. Toby had always been clingy, but now he whined every time I was out of his sight when I was still in the house.

Velma wanted to play guard dog. With Mark, it only happened when I first came home. She'd use her body as a blocker, not allowing him to get close to me. With other people, the hair on the back of her neck would stand up. The other day, when Russ and I had been having a disagreement, she'd even growled at him.

I'd reprimanded her for it because I didn't want to reward aggression, but it also eased the constant knot in my gut to know that if I ever needed her to defend me, she would.

Mark motioned me to the table. He'd already set out all the toppings and buns—tucked toward the middle of the table so the dogs couldn't steal one—and now he brought over a plate with the patties.

I stacked two slices of provolone on my burger—one for me and one for the baby. "I think Velma's not the only one trying to protect me."

I tried to keep my voice casual so Mark wouldn't catch on that I was fishing. He seemed like the most likely candidate for hiring Hal to follow me around. Even though he'd defended my abilities and independence to Russ, he worried about me, too. For all I knew, secretly hiring someone had been his way of placating Russ without making me angry.

Mark popped a slice of tomato into his mouth before answer-

ing. It was one of his quirks that I'd come to appreciate. He always
cut extra tomato so we could eat it fresh as well as on our burgers.

"You mean other than Russ?" he asked.

Which wasn't exactly a definitive answer. It might mean he
was dodging. It also might mean that he knew Russ was behind
it but didn't want to admit to it directly. Or it could mean he had
no idea what I was talking about and he thought someone else
had lectured me about staying safe now that I was pregnant.

With anyone else, I would have tried to come at it from a
different angle, assuming they'd lie to me if I asked them directly.

With Mark, he'd tell me the truth. The key was to ask him in
such a way that he couldn't evade my question while still being
honest. I told him about Hal tagging along. "I think someone
hired him to accompany me whenever I'm working a case. You
don't know anything about that, do you?"

Mark chewed his bite of burger at half speed, giving me time
to watch his expression. No signs of guilt. He looked more like
he was thinking.

At least that let me know he wasn't Hal's benefactor.

He swallowed his food. "Russ is the obvious choice. But I'm
guessing that's expensive. I don't know if Russ would or could
pay that kind of money for any length of time."

I ate a tomato slice before allowing myself another slice of
cheese. As part-owner of Sugarwood, Russ was comfortable, but
not wealthy. That said, it turned out he was also part of the

reason Sugarwood was financially successful. He was frugal to the point of being cheap.

Would he have felt it was important enough to spend that kind of money to have someone tag along after me all day?

I wasn't sure of the answer, but I had a feeling Mandy would know. Whatever was going on between her and Russ, they seemed to be spending a lot of time together. Romantic or not, she'd likely be the one he confided in when it came to something sneaky like that. He certainly wouldn't tell Stacey. I'd thought he would have told Mark, but perhaps he'd assumed Mark would tell on him.

We finished our meal and the ice cream sandwiches Mark had picked up for dessert.

Since Mark had to review some files before he testified in court again tomorrow on another case, it gave me the perfect time to call Mandy.

"So I have a suspicion about something," I said when she answered. "And I want you to tell me if you think I'm right or not."

She giggled. It bordered on nervous-guilty. "You know I love a good conspiracy theory."

For a while, after an employee was murdered in her bed and breakfast, I'd thought she'd been cured of her love of all things mystery, but the break had only been temporary. A zebra couldn't change its stripes, as the old cliché went.

I told her about how my firm's private investigator had offered to follow me on my case.

"Does he have a crush on you?" Mandy said. "You should make sure to flash him those beautiful rings Mark gave you."

Only Mandy would go straight for the romance angle. All the nervousness that I'd thought I'd sensed in her voice before had vanished. Maybe I'd simply caught her off-guard or pulled her out of a conversation where she'd been talking about me. Elise had told me that Mandy's favorite story, even months later, was about pulling me from the ground. And it seemed like every month that she told it, I was closer to death than I had been the previous month. Pretty soon she'd add in a detail about administering CPR while they waited for the EMTs.

Her continually re-telling that story could be a major contributor to Russ' anxiety about my safety.

"He's married, and he knows I'm both married and pregnant. I was thinking maybe someone paid him to follow me around and keep me safe..."

I let the sentence hang in the air without directly coming out and asking if she knew anything about it.

"I could see Mark doing something like that." She'd lowered her voice as if Mark were in the house with her rather than with me. "I don't know if he could handle losing his wife and baby a second time."

Her voice had that excited tone that it got when she thought she'd hit on the solution to a puzzle. If she genuinely thought

Mark had done it, then she couldn't have knowledge that Russ had hired Hal.

I settled into our couch and propped my feet up. My whole body immediately felt better. I didn't want to think about how I'd feel a few more months down the road. "Mark couldn't hide that for very long."

"You both have separate credit cards, don't you? And he pays the bills."

Technically, yes. Mark liked balancing budgets, and I hated it, so he'd taken over paying both our bills when we got married. But it wasn't Mark. He was the one person I was sure hadn't done it. Mark had a lot of skills. Lying wasn't one of them. Especially not lying to me.

"I was thinking Russ. Do you think it could be Russ?"

Mandy paused, and I could imagine her tapping her finger to her lips. "He hasn't said anything to me."

Toby dropped down next to the couch and laid his head on his paws, staring up at me. I stroked his ears. "Do you think he would have?"

"No doubt about it. He's been talking non-stop about how worried he is about you, and that hasn't changed in the last few days. It probably would have if he'd done something about it."

Mandy was right there. If Russ' behavior hadn't changed, then he wasn't the one behind my new bodyguard.

I might as well use Mandy's proclivity to theories to my

advantage while I had her. "If you had to guess who did it, who would you guess?"

"Other than Mark and Russ?"

"Other than Mark and Russ."

"I bet all the staff at Sugarwood pooled their money. If anything happens to you, Russ'll give himself a heart attack."

The image of everyone meeting in the sugar shack and passing around one of the sap buckets to take a collection flittered through my head. I snort-laughed. While the Sugarwood staff had proven to be loyal to both Russ and me—partly thanks to their memories of my Uncle Stan—that theory was less likely than that Mark was behind it all.

Hal had seemed unconcerned by how much time he'd spend with me. That meant whoever was behind this didn't have a cap on their budget.

But if it wasn't Mark and it wasn't Russ, who was it?

12

I spent the next two days helping Russ and Stacey with planning for the movies in the woods. We finally sourced a screen and found a perfect spot for it, purchased ticket stubs, and reserved a popcorn maker. Nancy and I finalized the menu for what other items we'd sell at the concession stand. They were all maple-syrup themed to help promote Sugarwood maple syrup.

Mandy's assurances that Russ would have told her seemed to be right. He lectured me half the time we were together until I told him that I was having the private investigator associated with my law firm accompany me. Since that'd basically been what he wanted all along, I finally got peace.

By the time Sunday hit, I was more than ready to spend the morning in church and the afternoon at a barbeque with Mark's family. I subtly poked around to see if any of them knew about

Hal, but all that got me was heckling. Apparently, I held the family record for near-death experiences, and that was saying something since Mark's little brother Bobby was a homicide detective in Detroit.

THE BOX THAT THE BABY'S CRIB CAME IN TOOK UP A THIRD OF THE former guest room. Mark and Erik had already taken apart the bed that used to be in here and moved it down to the unfinished basement. Hopefully, the crib wouldn't be as large as the box once we got it assembled.

If we got it assembled. We'd already been at it for half an hour—too full after the barbeque to want supper when we got home—and it still looked nothing like a crib. Sitting here gave me a lot of time to think about Jordan's death. I kept coming back to the fact that there weren't any signs of a struggle. From what I knew of her, Jordan seemed like the kind of person who would fight back.

It was the segment of the puzzle that made the least sense because the toxicology report came back clean. Drugs would explain her lack of a struggle, but there weren't any drugs in her system.

I handed Mark the piece that the instructions said we should attach next. "Are there any drugs that don't leave a trace?"

Mark paused, a screwdriver in one hand. "All drugs leave a

trace of some kind." He motioned for me to hold up the instructions. His gaze skimmed over them, and he screwed the two parts together. "Are you thinking about your case, or is this more of a *for future reference* question?"

"The case. If Jordan's killer worked at Papyrus Medical and had an intimate knowledge of pharmacology, then it could explain why there weren't any signs of a struggle. The killer drugged her first, tied the noose around her neck, hauled her up to the height they thought looked right, and then tipped a chair over next to her. Except that the toxicology screen was clean. It's frustrating. I thought maybe someone with knowledge of different drugs might have found one that wouldn't leave anything behind."

I squinted at the instructions. All the font was small enough that even 20/20 vision wouldn't be enough to easily read it. I needed a magnifying glass. The pictures weren't much help, either. The next piece we needed, according to the diagram, could be either of two pieces spread out in front of us. If they couldn't be bothered to quality control their assembly instructions, why were we trusting them with our baby's safety?

I held the instructions up to Mark again. "Can you tell which one should be next?"

He looked between the booklet and the wooden bars. He picked the longer of the two. "Some drugs will break down into components that are normal in the human body. They won't show up on a conventional tox screen or they're easy to overlook because all their parts, once they break down, are ones you'd expect to find. That's as close as you can get to a drug that leaves no traces."

The medical examiner who filled in for Mark while we were on our honeymoon was new. "Is it possible your temp missed something like that?"

Mark was glaring at the pieces now. The piece in his hand didn't fit where it was supposed to. He picked up the other option. "It's possible. It's something less experienced MEs could overlook when the toxicology report came back because those situations are rare. There aren't many poisons that metabolize that way, and the average person wouldn't have access to them. It takes a specific niche of killer to know they exist and get their hands on them."

But someone who worked at a pharmaceutical company might fit that profile.

The second piece he tried didn't fit, either.

Mark snagged the instruction booklet. He flipped through the pages. "I think they have the pieces labeled wrong. That semi-long piece had an L on it, but it definitely doesn't fit with the other L pieces."

When we were picking out a crib, buying one that we could assemble together had seemed like such a fun idea. Like a way to make a special memory. *Seemed* being the key word. Now it just felt like drudgery, and I wasn't sure anything we built would hold together once we set the baby in it. Building things clearly wasn't either of our strengths. "Do you want to return it and buy a pre-assembled one?"

Relief flashed across Mark's face. He visibly tried to wipe it away, but he only ended up looking concerned. "Are you sure?"

I opened the plastic bag that the parts came in and held it out toward him so he could fill it. "I'd much rather spend our time looking at the toxicology results and seeing if there might have been something the other ME missed."

Mark leaned over, took both my cheeks in his hands, and kissed me. "I love it when you talk crime."

We took apart the partially assembled crib and repackaged it at twice the speed that we'd unpackaged it. The box was too heavy for Mark to carry himself, and I wasn't supposed to be lifting anything heavy. He sent a text to Russ asking him to send a couple of the workers over on Monday morning to help load it back into his truck.

Mark looped my fingers through his. He led me to the couch, and we sat side by side. Times like this always reminded me of the first case we'd worked together when we were trying to figure out who killed my Uncle Stan. The circumstances were sad, but the memory itself always made me smile. Mark and I had always made a good team.

He flipped open his laptop. "I should be able to remotely access her toxicology report. That way I can see if any of her levels were elevated, and we can start adding potential drugs to our list."

I leaned my head against his shoulder and closed my eyes. I was allowed access to the toxicology report just like the prosecution. It was the defense's right to see all the evidence and have it independently assessed if we so chose. That said, I hadn't officially requested the toxicology report. Besides, it wasn't like I'd understand the blood chemistry results.

If we found something, I'd officially request the tox screen so we could use it in court. Right now, all I wanted to know was whether it was possible Dexter Ruffalo had figured out a drug that he could use to subdue Jordan without leaving any obvious traces.

Mark's fingers made quiet tapping noises on the keys. Instead of holding down the arrow keys to scroll, he had this cute but annoying way of briefly hitting the down or up arrow.

"All normal so far." More tapping, then the sound stopped. "Minutely elevated levels of succinic acid and choline."

I started to ask what those were, but it didn't matter what they were or what roll they played in the body. All that mattered was what they could be byproducts of—the cause of the elevated levels.

"That could mean succinylcholine," Mark said before I could even ask. "Medical professionals call it SUX. It's mainly used when they need to intubate a patient, but it's also one of the three drugs used in lethal injections."

I shuddered and opened my eyes. "And the only trace it

would leave behind would be slightly elevated levels of succinic acid and choline?"

Mark nodded. "It's easy to overlook, especially since SUX is highly regulated."

It was the kind of drug your average teacher or construction worker couldn't have gotten a hold of, but one that someone at a pharmaceutical company might have been able to steal. Papyrus Medical was one of the largest pharmaceutical firms in the state. It was possible they even manufactured SUX at one of their sites. It was something I'd have Hal look into.

Assuming I wasn't getting ahead of myself. Just because SUX broke down into those components in the body didn't mean it was what we were looking at. There might be other reasons a person would have slightly higher-than-normal levels of succinic acid and choline in their body.

The surrounding evidence needed to fit before we concluded SUX was involved. Jordan was hung, and she showed signs of suffocation consistent with a hanging death. We were looking for a very specific kind of drug for that. Mark had said SUX was used in the lethal injection cocktail, as well as in the medical field. Jordan's cause of death wasn't poisoning.

Mark had also said that it was used when doctors needed to put a tube down a person's throat. That suggested it had a numbing or calming effect, at least at some dosage level. If it was a powerful enough effect, it could have been used to kill Jordan without leaving signs of a struggle.

"What does SUX do?" I asked. "Would it have made her relaxed enough that someone could have put the rope around her neck without signs of a struggle?"

Mark closed his laptop and slowly set it on the coffee table. "It'd do more than that. I'll spare you the gory details of how it works, but when you inject someone, all their muscles stop working. Including the ones used to breath. She could have asphyxiated while lying on the floor and then been hung after she was already dead. If the killer worked quickly, there'd have been no way to tell that she didn't suffocate from hanging."

My stomach felt warm and uncomfortable, like it often had in the past couple of months right before I was sick. It was a good thing Mark had taken out the worst parts for me. What he did share was bad enough.

If she was already dead, or at least paralyzed, when she was strung up, it would explain why she hadn't grabbed at the rope, too.

We already knew that Dexter Ruffalo had motive. If some branch of Papyrus Medical produced SUX, that would be means. That left opportunity.

Since Jordan lived alone, all that would have taken was waiting for the right moment.

13

On Monday morning, my phone rang on my way back from walking the dogs after breakfast.

Hal's name flashed on my display.

I slid my finger across the screen to answer.

"Bad news," Hal said. "He's not our guy."

I stopped moving. Toby and Velma continued on for five feet before Velma looked back and stopped. Toby stopped a foot later. Pregnancy had some advantages. At one point, Velma had been so bad about running off that Mandy secretly bought her a collar with a GPS tracker in it. The dogs were so obsessed with not letting me out of their sight now that I didn't even have to worry about one of them getting too far away. It was like I'd been coated in bacon or something.

I turned my attention back to Hal's announcement. I'd been sure we'd find evidence that Dexter had been behind Jordan's faked suicide. Given his profession and the scam he'd almost gotten away with, he certainly had the intelligence and patience to pull something like her murder off. And he had the knowledge of drugs to know about SUX.

I thought about scowling at the phone, but I didn't want it coming through in my voice. It wasn't Hal's fault if I'd sent him chasing sensor echoes. "Are you sure?"

"One hundred percent, as long as you think the Grand Rapids police department can be trusted. He was locked up for disorderly conduct. He was dead drunk and urinated in public in front of a police officer."

Gross. I guess we knew how Dexter was taking his dismissal. The kind of person who went out and drunk himself into a stupor wasn't usually the same person who methodically plotted a murder, even if he hadn't had the best possible alibi.

Velma and Toby had stretched out on the ground in a puddle of sun. I sat down cross-legged between them. It probably wouldn't be long before my belly made getting up and down a challenge. I might as well enjoy it while I still could. Hopefully the warm sunshine would relax my brain and help me think.

"At least we won't waste any more time investigating him." On top of that, this path wasn't completely closed. Dexter couldn't have created an elaborate enough deception surrounding the new drug on his own. At least one other person had to have been involved. Maybe multiple people. And it wasn't likely the pharmaceutical company let those people off without some sort of repercussions. They'd have been fired if they also worked for Papyrus Medical. They'd have been reported to their superiors if they didn't. "We should look into whoever Dexter was working with to falsify the study results."

The noise of a mouse clicking came through the phone. "The company won't release that information without a fight, and it'll be hard to dig up otherwise. Do you think Andrea might speak to you privately?"

It was worth a try. "I'll give her a call and let you know." Since I'd come up empty-handed figuring out who'd hired Hal to follow me around, I might as well ask him. At the very least, I could confirm that he'd indeed been paid by someone and that it wasn't merely my paranoia talking. "One more thing before you go. Who paid you to go with me the other day?"

The clicking of his mouse stopped. "What gave me away?"

He was an honest enough man to own up to it. "There wasn't any one thing. It was more that recognizing inconsistencies is what I do."

A sound like a faint chuckle.

Might as well throw a Hail Mary while I had him laughing. "I don't suppose you'd be willing to tell me who it was."

A full chuckle this time. "You know I can't do that."

There was only one more person I could think of. "Was it Anderson?"

"No."

But Anderson had definitely been aware of what was

happening. He'd be my next stop in trying to figure this out. In the meantime… "As much as I appreciate the sentiment of whoever's behind this, you don't need to keep doing it. You have more important things to work on."

"All due respect, ma'am, the people who hired me don't think so. And I think I was an asset last week."

He had me there. I couldn't have posed as Jordan's family nearly as well without Hal there acting as Zach. Even though we were discovered, we wouldn't have gotten in the door without that ploy.

"Besides," Hal said, "I get a bonus for every week you don't figure it out and kick me off the case."

I wanted to snort the way I had on the phone with Mandy, but Mandy was my friend and Hal was a co-worker. I swallowed it down.

That seemed fair enough. If whoever hired him wanted me protected and were willing to offer a bonus, then why shouldn't Hal collect? "Fair enough. I'll let you know what I find out from Andrea."

At which point I might need a bodyguard after all. If the other people who'd been involved didn't have the same irrefutable alibi that Dexter did, we'd need to talk to them.

And regardless of how reckless Russ thought I was, I wasn't stupid enough to go talking to potential murderers alone.

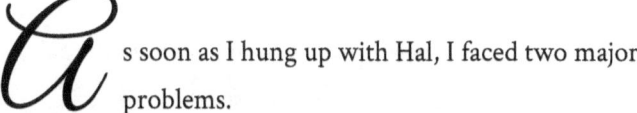s soon as I hung up with Hal, I faced two major problems.

I didn't have Andrea's phone number. And I didn't have her last name.

Her uncle was Martin Raymes, so there was a chance her last name was Raymes as well. I did a quick search on my phone for any Andrea Raymes in Michigan. No luck.

That meant all I knew about her for sure was she'd been Jordan's friend and she worked in the lab at Papyrus Medical.

Trying to call her at Papyrus Medical wouldn't get me anywhere. Not only was it possible that more than one Andrea worked there, but she wouldn't want to talk at work. She'd proven that with how clandestine she'd been about giving me Dexter's name in the elevator.

If I had Jordan's phone and her passcode, I could easily look through her contacts. Unfortunately, the police had her phone in evidence. They weren't going to release it to me and give me the code to go along with it.

What I did have was a list of Jordan's incoming and outgoing calls over the months before her death. It'd be tedious, but Andrea's number had to be among them. I could use a reverse look-up online on the numbers until I found hers. And pray that she was listed. Not everyone was anymore.

Part of me wanted to stay sitting in the sun with my dogs. It was the part of me that loved the peace of Sugarwood over the rush of Washington, DC.

The other part of me was already running on my internal hamster wheel, anxious to find out what else Andrea knew.

The dogs and I headed back. I got them each a bowl of fresh water and then settled in with the phone records and my laptop on the couch.

I started by organizing all the numbers Jordan had called or who'd called her so that I didn't miss one and didn't keep looking up the same number more than once.

Then I pulled up the reverse look-up page and got started.

She had the kind of calls I would have expected. She talked to Zach a couple of times a week. She talked to a woman who shared their last name a couple of times a month—likely an aunt or a cousin, since their mother was dead.

The usual calls you'd expect from someone dealing with their father's estate also played a major role. She'd been talking to an accountant—probably dealing with death taxes—and with a place that inscribed headstones.

There were a couple of calls with men whose names didn't have an immediate, clear connection to Jordan. She'd also called a newspaper in Grand Rapids, maybe for her dad's obituary, though it seemed too long after his death for that.

Halfway through my list I hit on a number belonging to an Andrea Ferris. Her CEO uncle must be a maternal uncle since they didn't share a last name.

I glanced at the clock. She'd still be at work now, but I could leave a message for her to call me when she was done. If I didn't hear from her by seven o'clock tonight, I'd try again.

I dialed her number and waited.

"Hello?" a woman's voice said.

I'd been so prepared for her voicemail that, for a second, my brain struggled to process that a live person picked up instead.

"Hello?" she said again.

If I started in by asking if she was Andrea, she could think I was a telemarketer. I'd been hung up on before when Case Hammond mistook me for one. I'd open differently this time.

"It's Nicole Fitzhenry-Dawes. Zach Williams' lawyer. Is this Andrea?"

"Yes." The fact that I wasn't a telemarketer after all hadn't gotten rid of the hint of suspicion in her voice. "How did you get this number?"

"It was in the record of Jordan's calls."

Her end of the line went quiet. Mine would have, too, had the situation been reversed. Telling her I'd gotten her number from Jordan's phone log couldn't help but remind her that her friend was gone and that she wouldn't be talking to her anymore.

The silence on her end was too complete, though. If she were at work, there should have been some sound behind her. None of the rooms I'd been in other than Lisa's office had been that level of quiet.

Maybe that's why she wasn't saying anything more. Maybe she was with someone and she didn't want to let on who I was.

I'd give her a question she could answer with a yes or no.

"Is this a good time to talk?"

"It'll never be a good time." Andrea huffed out a small breath. "But you didn't catch me at work, if that's what you mean."

It'll never be a good time? That was a bit strange. Did she still think Zach had killed Jordan? Even after giving me Dexter's name?

She might have given me his name not because she believed Dexter killed Jordan but because she believed I wanted the truth.

Regardless, all I could do now was come in directly and see how it went. "My private investigator found out that Dexter couldn't have been involved in Jordan's death."

Another short pause, almost like she was sitting down. "I'm not surprised. Dexter's the kind of person who'd cheat on his taxes. He's not the kind who'd take part in a revenge killing. There's no profit in revenge."

So she'd given me Dexter's name as a just in case. She didn't think he'd done it, but she didn't want to take the chance.

As I'd suspected, what we had in common was we both wanted the truth about Jordan's death.

"I still think her death could be related to the falsified study results. Was there anyone else involved?"

"Dexter was the ringleader."

Last week, when I'd talked to her and Lisa, I'd never gotten the feeling like she was trying to hide something from me. I got it now. Her answer wasn't really an answer. It only played one on TV, if I could adapt the saying to my own purposes.

Time to phrase it in a way that she couldn't sidestep. "Was anyone else fired or disciplined in relation to the falsified studies?"

Andrea's end of the line went quiet again, this time for long enough that I was afraid she was considering hanging up on me.

She blew out another little breath. "One other man was fired, and two others were suspended. But I can't give you their names."

I put a star beside the numbers and names on Jordan's call log that didn't have a known connection to her. It was possible they belonged to one of the other people.

Andrea's answer held another small dodge, though. She obviously knew the names of the people involved. She'd taken part in the investigation.

Which meant she couldn't share them for another reason. If

that reason had a weak foundation, I might still be able to get the names from her. Then all I'd have to do would be to match them to someone who called Jordan and we'd have a viable new lead.

"I can keep it anonymous that you were my source for the names. And it would help my investigation a lot to have them. One of them might have played a part in Jordan's death."

"The two who were suspended confessed when they learned about the investigation. We didn't discover the part they played on our own." Andrea's tone said *please understand*. "And even if I wanted to tell you the name of the other lab tech who was fired over this, I couldn't. My job's on the line now. Not to mention my relationship with my family." Her voice dropped to almost a whisper on the last part, as if she was ashamed to admit it.

It didn't make sense. She'd been careful in slipping me Dexter's name. "You and Lisa got in trouble for telling us what happened?"

"Not only for that. Lisa's on probation, but they didn't suspend her. Somehow they found out that I gave you Dexter's name."

The apology was gone from her voice now.

I sucked in a deep breath. Papyrus Medical must have a source in the police department. Once Hal started poking around, they'd put it together that either Lisa or Andrea had probably given us Dexter's name. Andrea seemed like an honest enough person that she wouldn't have lied if they asked her directly.

Or they might have figured it out thanks to all those mirrored walls in the elevator. She'd blocked the camera's direct view of us exchanging the note, but whoever reviewed the recording might have still been able to see what was happening in the reflection on the walls.

She needed to know that I hadn't revealed her as my source. "We didn't tell anyone where we got that name from."

She made a noise that sounded a lot like *uh-huh*. "Either way, it's now in my permanent record that I violated confidentiality. If my uncle wasn't the CEO, I'd be fired already."

I clearly couldn't promise her that no one would find out if she gave me the other names. No one should have found out she'd given me Dexter's name, but they had.

And I wasn't going to pressure her. Losing a job—and potentially having to look for another one without anyone from the last one serving as a reference—was career suicide in the current job climate.

But I did want to make sure she didn't regret this later. "I'm only asking because I think it's important that we find out who killed Jordan. They might come after you next."

I could almost see her shaking her head across the miles. "No one has threatened me or contacted me, and finding out who killed Jordan is the police's job. They think it was Zach. Maybe it wasn't. Maybe it was. I couldn't tell you why, but I wasn't surprised when I heard he'd been charged." She let out a full length sigh this time. "Besides, my uncle called my mom from overseas. I got a lecture from my dad about how disappointed he is in me for breaking the law, and my mom cried all afternoon because my uncle had to put himself on the line to save me. I can't cross that bridge again."

The truth felt like it hit my brain in a little flash. Had this just been a simple case of finding Jordan's killer, she would have risked her job for it. She wouldn't risk her relationship with her family. Her lowered voice earlier was because she was ashamed that her family mattered so much to her. She'd cared about Jordan, but Jordan was gone. Her family was still here, and she was going to protect them and her role within their ecosystem, regardless of the cost. She'd trust the police to deal with it from now on.

All I had left to say was, "I'm sorry for how this turned out."

"Me too," Andrea said, and then she disconnected the call before I could.

I couldn't blame her for putting her family first over finding her friend's killer. I wouldn't try to contact her again.

Her words about Zach kept playing over and over in my mind. I needed to talk to him again. Not only to see if he could identify any of the remaining names on my phone call list, but also to see if I could find out why Andrea would have believed it when the police said he'd killed Jordan.

I didn't want to go through all of this only to find out that I'd provided enough reasonable doubt to allow a murderer to walk free.

*a*ndrea's concerns about Zach had gotten deep enough inside my head that I didn't feel comfortable inviting him to my house. It was silly. He said he was innocent. Even if he wasn't, he was my client with no reason to hurt me. Velma would have been there, and she certainly wouldn't have let him hurt me.

But I wasn't willing to take the risk. Especially not when doing so would prove Russ right that I was only thinking of myself and not thinking about my baby.

Instead, I made an appointment to meet with him at the office. That's what it was for, after all.

We met the next day, first thing in the morning, after he got off the night shift.

He looked different than the first time I met him. Worse. His skin had the pasty look of someone who hadn't been out in the sun after a long winter, despite the fact that this had been an unseasonably warm May. It was like we'd skipped most of spring and went straight from winter to summer. The news blamed it on global warming.

I couldn't imagine the toll working in an emergency room must take on a person. Each day you'd see the worst of what happened in the world. The potential trauma from that wouldn't be as bad as what first responders experienced, but it'd only be one step down.

Thankfully, he'd changed out of his scrubs. Unfortunately, he still had that strange antiseptic smell clinging to him.

I led him back to my office and set the list of names down on the desk in front of him. I'd taken the phone numbers off.

I took my spot on the other side of my desk, but the smell of disinfectant felt like it wrapped around my throat, trying to choke me. It hadn't seemed this strong out in the open area of reception. In the smaller space of my office, it clogged up my nose so I could barely breathe.

An overly warm sensation rose up in my throat, and I swallowed rapidly. Now was not the time to be sick to my stomach again.

One of the tricks I'd developed was to keep my mind active. Staring at him while he read the names on the paper didn't fit the bill.

I coughed to loosen my throat. "The prosecution will be calling anyone to the stand who might know of a reason you would want to kill Jordan. They'll give us a list of names, but they won't tell us what they know. Can you think of anyone who might believe you would kill Jordan?"

He stopped writing next to one of the names on the paper. He'd jotted the word *aunt* next to the woman's name who shared their last name.

"Unless they're going to dredge up sibling rivalry or that we sometimes disagreed over what to do with our father's estate, they won't find a motive." His voice was level, almost monotone. "I thought we covered that already."

In a way, we had, but I hadn't looked into his case myself yet at that point. Now I'd met Andrea.

"I was talking to…" Andrea's name stuck to my tongue and didn't want to release. There was no law that said I had to tell my client everything I'd looked into as a possible defense. I didn't want to get Andrea into any more trouble than I already had. "To a friend of Jordan's, and she was very open about not being surprised when you were arrested for Jordan's murder."

He wrote a question mark beside another name and then glanced up at me. "Was it Andrea?"

He broke his gaze away and redirected it back to the page.

The feeling that he'd cracked open my skull and looked at the secrets inside wouldn't go away. I forced a smile onto my lips, but I couldn't make it reach my eyes no matter how hard I tried. Hopefully at least trying to smile would keep my voice light. "Good guess."

A hint of a smile played on his lips. "Good deduction. I told you about problems Jordan was having at work. A good lawyer would look around her workplace, and Andrea was a co-worker of Jordan's. It made sense."

He didn't flinch at all when he said Jordan's name now. It came across as cold. We'd have to work on that before he took the stand.

Right now, I needed to know why Andrea felt the way she did. "Do we need to be worried that she knows something?"

He made a note next to the last name on the list. "Not unless my views on abortion and physician-assisted suicide could count as motive." He pushed my paper and pen back to me. "I've seen a lot after working so long in a hospital setting, and I'm pro-choice on both accounts. Andrea took the opposite side. It's why there was no second date." His lips edged up at the corners. "No doubt she thinks someone who would abort fetuses and allow terminally ill patients to end their life doesn't value life at all."

A pulsating twitch a bit like a mild muscle spasm hit my stomach, and I rubbed at the spot where I imagined my baby napped.

Hearing Zach call a baby a fetus made me want to wrap both arms around my stomach and shield him or her. It was silly. He wasn't threatening him or her just because he believed abortion might be the right choice in some cases, but I couldn't seem to control my reaction. My baby wasn't born yet—and was well within the legal timeframe for abortion in many places—but I loved him or her so much already. To Zach, that's probably what made my baby valuable. He or she was wanted.

At least he'd explained away Andrea's reaction to him. No one would put her on the stand to argue something general like that. I'd object, and the judge wouldn't allow the testimony to continue.

We needed to worry about people who could present some sort of a concrete motive.

The muscle spasm pulse in my stomach didn't let up. I rubbed in a wider circle. It was probably nothing. I needed to focus, and it would pass. "What did you and Jordan disagree about when it came to your father's estate?"

"What to do with some of what he left behind." His gaze had lasered in on me, and his posture tightened. "Are you alright?"

He wasn't a doctor, but he was a nurse, and he worked in the ER. He'd probably seen pregnant women a hundred times where they'd panicked over something that was nothing. Telling him could put me in that same camp, but my doctor had said not to be afraid to ask if something worried me.

I laid my other hand on my belly. "I'm having a strange feeling where the baby is."

His shoulders eased. "You're in your second trimester, I'd guess. It's probably just the baby moving for the first time."

My heart pounded hard enough in my chest that I could feel the movement. The sensation in my stomach couldn't be the baby moving. That happened about a week ago, even though the doctor said with a first baby I might not feel movement until twenty weeks or later. "That was more like flutters. This is more rhythmic."

Zach was on his feet. He took my wrist, his fingers on the spot where my pulse beat. "Your heart rate's high. Are you in pain?"

I shook my head. It didn't hurt.

It also didn't feel normal.

"Should I go to the hospital?"

Zach helped me to my feet. "It wouldn't hurt to get checked out."

The floor felt a little unsteady under my feet.

It's because you're panicking, the logical voice that sounded like my mom said. *That has nothing to do with the baby.*

I quickly swept my paperwork into my bag.

Zach kept a hand under my elbow, as if he knew I was unsteady on my feet. Andrea might have assumed from his political views that he didn't value life, but she had to be wrong. He seemed to value my life and my baby's life right now, though that might have only been because I was the one trying to make sure he didn't spend the rest of his behind bars.

Anderson came out of his office as we walked past it. He took one look at my face and froze. "What's going on?"

"I'm taking her to the hospital," Zach said. "You might want to call her husband."

16

*E*lise reached me before Mark did.

"Mark's on his way, but he's at the far end of the county," she said. "I told Anderson and the creepy guy with him that they didn't have to wait."

The extra-fluffy tone of her voice and her nicknaming of Zach said she was trying to distract me. It wasn't working, but I appreciated the effort.

The weird stomach pulses had stopped, but I still felt like throwing up—only this time it wasn't morning sickness. It was fear. If anything happened to this baby, Mark might be too afraid to try again.

I might be too afraid to try again.

All of a sudden, all I wanted was a mom. My mom. Mark's mom. But my mom was over six hundred miles away, and Mark's parents had gone camping for the week.

I silently patted the examination table where I was perched, waiting for the ultrasound machine and the doctor.

Elise hopped up beside me, and I leaned into her.

We stayed that way until the doctor came in with the nurse. The nurse wanted Elise to leave, but I wasn't letting go of her hand, so they were out of luck. It wasn't like she'd never seen a bare belly before.

Five minutes and a lot of cold goo later, the doctor smiled at me.

"Everything with the baby looks fine. Based on what I'm seeing and your description, I think it was a simple case of the hiccups."

Elise did the Cavanaugh eyebrow raise at him. "All due respect, but I've been pregnant twice, and I've never heard of unborn babies getting hiccups."

He switched the ultrasound machine off. "It doesn't happen to everyone. We think it can sometimes be linked to the baby's lungs developing." He shifted to face me. "It's nothing to worry about unless it starts happening more than once a day. Try to keep a watch on it."

How could I do anything but? If the baby did that more than once a day, I wouldn't be able to concentrate on anything else. I hadn't even glanced at the sheet of names I'd had Zach working on, despite sitting alone in this room for at least ten minutes before Elise got here.

I'd been so distracted that I hadn't even considered sneakily getting the doctor to tell me the sex of the baby without Mark finding out. Motherhood was making me lose my edge.

ON THE DRIVE BACK TO THE OFFICE, I CALLED MARK AND LET him know that everything was okay so that he didn't drive faster than he should. Elise insisted on following me home from there to make sure I was safe.

She even offered to stay with me until Mark got home, but now that the "crisis" was over, all I wanted to do was read the notes Zach made next to the names from Jordan's call list.

I'd shoved it into my bag so haphazardly that it was more of a ball than a sheet when I took it out.

I smoothed it flat on the kitchen table.

Zach had managed to narrow it down significantly. Only three names still left questions in my mind.

Beside one, he'd written *She worked with him. I think they dated for a couple of months.*

Beside two other names—one a man's and one a woman's—he'd left question marks.

I snapped my fingers. Because of the baby's hiccups, I'd forgotten to ask Zach about the call Jordan made to the newspaper office. I'd looked up their father's obituary, and it'd been published long before the call she made in her final month. It'd also been placed in an entirely different newspaper.

It made me think that perhaps she hadn't been as convinced that Papyrus Medical planned to properly deal with the new drug. She might have been in contact with a reporter. If I was right, it meant she was scared, even if Andrea didn't know it. She might have given all the information she'd collected to a reporter to publish if she felt the company was still hiding something.

If that was the case, a good reporter should have been suspicious after Jordan's death. They should have been nosing around, and perhaps asking the same question I was asking. Was Jordan's death connected to her work?

The problem was that a lot of people worked at the newspaper she'd called. Figuring out which reporter she might have been dealing with would be a new hurdle for us. Assuming my baby didn't hiccup anymore or sneeze or whatever else babies could do before they were born that I didn't know about, figuring out who Jordan was talking to at the newspaper and how she was connected to the names Zach didn't recognize would be the next task Hal and I needed to tackle.

After my scare today, having Hal tag along with me seemed like an even better idea. If I found out who'd hired him, I might even thank them.

17

The baby hiccups must have scared Mark more than he let on. The next morning, he served me breakfast in bed and sat next to me while I ate, his hand on my stomach. When we were together, it was easy to forget that either of us had a past. So often it felt like there'd only ever been us. At times like this, though, the room we were in was crowded with his deceased wife and daughter and my mom, who'd wanted two children, but had only ever been able to have me.

We didn't talk about the two babies she miscarried when I was too young to even know what was happening. I still wouldn't know about them if my Uncle Stan hadn't told me. My parents' silence on the subject didn't surprise me. My mom probably saw losing those babies as a failure on her part, even though nothing could have been further from the truth. But, for whatever reason, her body refused to carry any more babies to term, and imperfection wasn't something my parents tolerated. They preferred to pretend nothing had happened.

Mark left for work, and I dressed for a day spent around Sugarwood. We only had a couple weeks remaining before our Movies in the Woods. I had to meet with Nancy. We planned to have bottles of maple syrup there for purchase, and Nancy felt she could make maple candies and her maple-butter filled cookies in advance, but we needed to see if we could reproduce in bulk the maple syrup popcorn I'd created for Stacey's baby shower. Nancy wanted to do a version with nuts and without.

I tucked the dogs into their crates and grabbed my purse. My phone rang before I was out the door.

Hal.

That was quick work. I'd only sent him the names and phone numbers last night.

I answered. "Are you sure you're not neglecting other cases to focus on this one?"

"You have my word," Hal said. "The extra work is actually a favor right now. My wife and kids are down in Arizona, visiting her family, so if I'm not working, I spend my evenings eating Hamburger Helper in front of the TV."

That was an odd mental image. I couldn't envision Hal either eating Hamburger Helper or watching TV. Having a lot of time to fill made sense if he was used to his free time being taken up by a wife and kids.

"The coworker she dated still works at Papyrus Medical, and he was out with his new girlfriend when Jordan died."

Hal switched topics so quickly that my brain worked double-time to catch up. "And the other two?"

"The woman, Coleen Uphill, is editor-in-chief for the *Courier Press* out of Grand Rapids. I'll text you her information once we're done."

That was the same newspaper that Jordan had called. My theory that everything wasn't as rosy as it seemed at Papyrus Medical looked more likely all the time.

If it turned out that the third name belonged to the other person who was involved with the scam, I'd be certain of it.

"Otto Corder is a strange one," Hal said.

Hal's pause felt like it was long and drawn out for effect even though it wasn't any longer than the break between the first and the second names.

"He doesn't seem to have any connection to Papyrus Medical or to Jordan that I can tell."

Zach hadn't recognized his name, so he wasn't a family friend or a family member.

If I assumed that Jordan was digging deeper into the business practices of her employers, then maybe he was part of a study that had been done on another drug—one that was already on the market. That was information I couldn't find out on my own. "I'll take care of calling the reporter, but I need you to dig deeper into Otto Corder. Specifically, did he ever participate in a medical study?"

We disconnected, and my phone dinged. The direct phone number for Coleen Uphill from Hal.

It'd be nice if we could finally catch a break on this case. Even though Zach insisted he was innocent, and he had a reasonable explanation for why Andrea thought he was guilty, her reaction niggled at me.

The jury could interpret Zach the same way she had. He did come across as cold and calculating at times. Juries were only people, and they did tend to judge on first impressions and gut instincts as well as the facts. It was why my parents required their clients to wear clothes they'd selected for them.

I'd feel better about the whole situation if we could establish a strong link between the corruption at Papyrus Medical and Jordan's death. Whether the prosecutor moved to drop charges or not, we'd have a much better chance of winning when the case went to trial if we could show Jordan's death had a reasonable chance of being linked to her work situation.

I was supposed to meet with Nancy in less than ten minutes, but it was a short walk there. I didn't want to try to call on the way since I'd inevitably walk through a dead zone and lose the call at the worst possible moment.

I tapped the number in Hal's text and let the phone dial.

"Coleen Uphill, *Courier Press*."

The woman's voice had a deep quality to it, like her lungs

had been scarred by too many packs of cigarettes and long nights. Almost like she belonged in a different era of reporters.

"My name's Nicole Fitzhenry-Dawes." I'd give the barest of details and see what she said. "I'm investigating the death of Jordan Williams."

Coleen made a noise like she was unsuccessfully trying to clear something from the very bottom of her throat. "Yeah. That was too bad. I only met her a couple of times, but she seemed like a nice kid. Very earnest."

Referring to Jordan as a "nice kid" pegged her as significantly older.

"What can I do to help you?" she asked.

My shoulders wanted to dip. If she had to ask, the chances that Jordan had confided in her about something nefarious happening at Papyrus Medical dipped to infinitesimal.

Unless she was worried I was from Papyrus Medical and I was trying to find out who Jordan might have told so that I could get rid of them, too.

Not many people would think like that—other than me—but Coleen was a reporter. She might have the same suspicious tendencies.

I wouldn't give up yet. "I'm following up on the places she went and the people she talked to prior to her death. What was Jordan contacting you about?"

"Our archives. We're not a big enough paper for the library to want to house them, so she came here to the basement."

With all that Jordan had been dealing with around losing her dad and outing a corrupt co-worker, why would she spend her spare time reading through newspaper archives in Grand Rapids?

"Do you know what she was looking for?"

"Nope. But if you want to come by this week, I can set you up to look at the year she was interested in."

Why not? That, at least, I could do without needing Hal, freeing him up to chase down the information I couldn't.

I set up a time to meet Coleen at the *Courier Press* building.

If Jordan had been merely a history fan, she could have read books or even watched one of the historical recreation channels on YouTube.

Whatever she'd been looking for in the Courier Press archives had to be important. The only question was whether it was important to unraveling the secret behind why she'd been killed.

18

The moment I stepped into the basement of the *Courier Press* where the archives were stored, I wished I hadn't come alone. The lights were bare bulbs surrounded by caging, and they gave off a dim yellow glow that cast sketchy shadows across Coleen's face.

It was the kind of location where, had it appeared in a horror movie, I would have been shouting at the characters not to go in.

But this wasn't a horror movie. Jordan hadn't been killed here. And Coleen was the exact opposite of a threat. She stood five feet tall, with a waist as thin as my arms. The wrinkles covering her face suggested she was nearing retirement age. She might have already passed it. She struck me as the kind of person who wanted to die at their desk.

She stood on her tiptoes and pulled on the string of a hanging lamp. It burst into light. I squinted against it.

It illuminated a desk with a machine on it that looked like a computer that would have been around before I was born. Why would they make people come down here to access the archives when they had much newer computers upstairs? For that matter, why not just upload them all so they were accessible online?

The dinosaur computer didn't seem to have a keyboard.

Wait a second... "Is this a microfiche machine?"

"Microfilm actually," Collen said. "Let me grab you the reel Jordan looked at when she was here."

She went over to a tall filing cabinet with narrow drawers and pulled out a box. She dumped a round object that looked like a hand-sized version of an old film reel into her palm.

She came back to my side. "Do you know how to work one of these?"

I shook my head. If I was being honest, I didn't even know anyone used them anymore. I thought most things had been digitized by this point. Maybe that showed my age.

"Jordan didn't, either. What's the world coming to?" She slid the reel onto a metal rod and snapped the end of the film into a holder. She pressed a button, and the screen came to life, displaying the first issue of that year. She pointed at a blue knob. "Right is forward. Left is back. The farther you turn it, the faster it goes." She poked a thumb back over her shoulder. "I'll be upstairs if you need me."

And with that, she left me alone in the creepy lair that

seemed like it should have belonged to Victor Frankenstein's literary cousin.

It's a basement in a business, I reminded myself. *It's not a haunted house.*

I glanced at the date on the issue again. It was from over thirty-five years ago.

This might turn out to be a complete waste of time. Jordan wasn't a reporter. She was a pharmaceutical rep. Unless she suspected her company was founded by a Nazi or that they'd been secretly making people sick only to cure them for three decades, this seemed like it wouldn't have much to do with her death.

But she had come here and spent a whole day, the same as I was, reading through old newspapers.

The first issue of that year didn't have anything more interesting than that the New Year's baby was the second of twins. The first baby was born one minute before midnight, giving them different birthdays.

I moved on to the next issue and then the next. Maybe because it was a smaller paper, they seemed to cover more quirky items—like the theft of a newly planted peach tree from a woman's front yard and the newest kids' toys that were equally fun for adults. They also seemed to cover bigger stories in more depth, sometimes following them for weeks or months at a time, chasing theories. They followed up on stories long after the bigger papers had moved on to more current events. By the end

of the year, they'd even created a recurring section for it where
they specifically revisited an old news story and updated readers
on where things stood.

The overarching stories that took up the most pages were
about a Jane Doe's body that washed up from the Grand River
next to Riverside Park, an armored car robbery of Ironclad
Armored Car Services, and a series of joyrides taking place across
the city. The joyrider only stole pickup trucks and returned them
covered in mud.

I checked the byline. Most of them were written by Coleen.
Apparently, she'd risen to her place as editor-in-chief through
finding a niche for the *Courier Press* that was different from
what the other newspapers were doing. That might even be why
such a small paper had managed to last so long in an ever-
shrinking market. Most people I knew got their news from
online sources.

The Jane Doe articles were actually really interesting. Coleen
had followed up with the police as to whether it was a murder or
a suicide—they suspected suicide but couldn't be certain. From
there, she personally dug into missing persons' reports, trying to
identify the Jane Doe herself.

In November of that year, she succeeded. Jane Doe turned
out to be a woman named Anna. She was a schizophrenic who
had a history of going on and off her meds. When she was off,
she lived on the streets. Her pattern of disappearing was why her

family didn't report her missing immediately. They assumed she'd turn up the way she always had before.

None of that had any connection to Jordan that I could see.

Nor did anything else in the papers.

I even went back and read the classifieds and obituaries. I took a picture of any that included a person with the last name Williams. Since most of them were people selling furniture and renting apartments, the chances that they'd somehow resulted in Jordan's death didn't seem high. But at least I'd have the images on my phone in case.

I scrolled back and snapped pictures of the quirkier articles and follow-ups that I thought the larger papers wouldn't have run as well. Jordan had specifically come here. The only reason I could see for that was that the *Courier Press* had covered something that the larger papers ignored.

I just had to figure out what it was.

19

The following day, I didn't have time to pursue what Jordan might have been looking for at all. Stacey and I had decided that we needed a trial run of Movies in the Woods before we officially opened up to the public. We'd decided to host a Saturday night movie for friends, family, and Sugarwood employees.

If something was going to go wrong, we wanted it to happen when the spots were filled with people who hadn't paid for the experience. It seemed like a nice way to thank our staff after an exceptionally long sugaring season, too.

Dave—our writer-in-residence who also ran our rental shop —arrived first. He carried two lawn chairs under his arms even though he was alone. Hopefully he hadn't progressed to believing his characters were real.

He waved at Stacey and swung one chair out as if to ask *Is here a good spot?*

The second chair must be for her.

After a long discussion between all of us, we'd decided to pitch the Movies in the Woods a bit like fireworks, where you needed to bring your own lawn chairs or blankets.

I smacked a mosquito off my arm.

And bug repellent.

Where was Mandy? She'd promised to bring all-natural bug repellent for me. The day after I invited her, she called me in a panic because she'd been reading about the dangerous toxins in most bug repellents, and she didn't think I should risk the baby.

I told her I'd be risking the baby more if I got West Nile from a mosquito bite or Lyme disease from a tick. Two hours later, she'd texted me that she'd bring me something safe.

I turned on my flashlight, even though it wasn't really dark enough for it yet. The garden lamps we'd set up to mark the path through the bush had only barely begun glowing. Despite that, it was dark enough out here for me to want more light. That seemed to be part of the city girl that I couldn't leave behind.

Mandy stood over by the concession cart with Mark. Her arms moved in big motions, almost like she was painting.

I called her name.

She jumped, and her hands flattened tight to her sides. She stepped back away from Mark.

It was a guilty move. Just like how she sounded like she was hiding something when I called to ask her if Russ had hired Hal. Even though she hadn't known anything about that, she'd still been nervous that I wanted to run a theory past her.

Her expression relaxed, and she pulled her bag up higher. She opened it wide and reached inside as if she'd just remembered that she'd promised me healthy bug spray and that was the most likely reason for me to be calling her name.

She lifted out a clear spray bottle like I used to mix vinegar and water in for cleaning. It was huge. She could spray the whole clearing with that amount. Hopefully that's not what she intended to do.

She said something to Mark, and he obediently held out his arms. If I knew Mandy, she'd come up with the idea that I shouldn't even be breathing the regular bug spray or coming into contact with it on him. She might plan to spray everyone who showed up with her concoction.

Elise and Erik—Arielle and Cameron with them—entered the clearing. Arielle was walking halfway backward, talking to a boy who looked to be about her age.

Hal and a woman came into view. The boy must be his. He held the hand of a little girl, and his wife carried a bundle.

I'd invited him because I thought he'd otherwise be stuck home alone again, but it looked like his family was back. It was a good thing we'd chosen *The Incredibles* as our first showing, thinking it'd be a good family-friendly option. Elise didn't expect Arielle and Cameron to stay awake through all of it, but she thought it'd be a fun treat for them anyway.

Hal passed the little girl's hand to his wife and headed in my direction.

"I got more information on Otto Corder," he said. "Still no clear connection to Jordan that I can tell."

Crap. Andrea would say we should stop looking because the police seemed to have found the right guy, but Zach had taken good care of me when I had my scare. I couldn't reconcile that with him being the kind of person who'd kill his sister.

You didn't think Peter was the kind of guy who'd kill his wife, either, and look how that turned out.

I shoved the suspicious voice to the back of my mind. "What did you find out?"

Hal did a head shake-shrug combo. "He's married. Retired. Lives outside Grand Rapids with his wife. His roses won a prize in last year's fair. He's never been in a clinical trial. In fact, he's not even taking any medication. The closest connection he has to the medical world is that his wife used to work as a receptionist at the hospital."

Maybe we'd made a wrong assumption. His name showed up on Jordan's phone, but that didn't mean he'd been the one to call. "What about his wife? Is she taking any medication?"

"None that showed up in my search. They're both healthy."

There went that idea. Okay, so maybe they weren't the subject. Maybe they knew something about how clinical trials could be falsified. Or they might have some other specialized knowledge. "Where did they work before they retired? Remind me?"

"She was a check-in desk receptionist at the hospital, and he drove an armored truck. Nothing to do with pharmaceuticals at all."

He drove an armored truck. That wasn't a career you often ran into, and I'd encountered armored trucks twice this week now.

My parents liked to tell me that coincidences could never be allowed to exist in a criminal case. They either needed to be explained away or exploited.

It seemed like too much to think that Jordan had been reading newspapers that featured an armored car robbery, and that she accidentally happened to also be talking to a man who used to drive an armored car for a living. I had no idea yet whether it connected to her work at Papyrus Medical or her death, but first I needed to confirm that it was a real connection.

"Did you find out what company he worked for?"

Hal's wife slid her arm through his. "You're not talking business, are you?"

He looked at me sidelong as if to say *Don't rat me out.*

"This is my wife, Margo," he said. "This is Nicole, Anderson's law partner."

Something flickered across her face, but in the dim light, I couldn't tell what exactly.

She tightened her grip on Hal's arm. "The extra work as bodyguard." She tilted her face up to look at him. "You're not on the clock now, are you?"

Ah. I got it. They had some stress over how much Hal worked. She must insist on a strict separation of work time and family time.

I held up my hands. "Completely social." I pointed toward Elise and Erik. "That's my cousin-in-law and her husband. They're both police officers. We're even expecting Fair Haven's chief of police and his wife tonight, so Hal's definitely off the clock."

She relaxed against him, and a smile softened her face.

I'd grown up in a family where my parents worked together and so they understood the demands of the job. Even Mark and I were in related fields. It must be so difficult to be in a marriage where one person's job added stress and made the other partner at least a little unhappy. Anderson was right about that. They wouldn't want to stand in the way of their partner doing what they enjoyed, but they'd also have to find some way to keep it from ruining their own joy in their life.

That must be where the separation of work and family came in for Hal and Margo.

If I was getting that name from Hal tonight—or even this weekend—I'd have to be subtle about it.

I motioned toward the concession stand. "Make sure to give

us feedback on what you like and what you wish we had. You're our guinea pigs tonight."

She laughed, and the rest of the tension came out of her upper body. "I did eye up that maple-syrup popcorn on our way in…"

She led Hal off.

A cold spritz hit my arm. I yelped, and it sounded a bit like a crazed hyena.

Mandy took hold of my hand and stretched my arm out. "It'll only feel cold for a second, and I promise it's better for the baby."

She aimed a second spray at my arm. I already smelled a bit like a lemon citronella candle. That was a step up from the chemical odor of normal bug sprays at least…though it was kind of making me hungry.

Mandy tilted her head toward where Hal and Margo stood at the concession cart. Nancy was explaining all the options to them.

"Is that the bodyguard that your mystery protector hired?" Mandy asked.

I nodded.

Mandy moved on to my other arm. "Have you told your parents about your bodyguard? I'm sure they'd be glad to hear it now that their grandchild is involved, too."

I stilled, and not only because it kept Mandy from spraying my clothes.

My parents wouldn't have, would they?

But even as I asked myself the question, I knew the answer. It was more than possible. I would have suspected them of hiring Hal sooner had I not been focused on it being someone here. That had been an assumption, one my parents had probably counted on me making.

I'd confirm my suspicions later. Right now, I had bigger cakes to bake.

Everyone had settled into their seats except for Mandy and me. Mark had lawn chairs waiting for both of us off to one side. Russ would be manning the projector.

Just like in a regular movie theater, we'd included a clip at the beginning that asked everyone to turn off their phones. If I wanted to know which company Otto worked for so that I could relax tomorrow, I had to get a text off to Hal before that played. I'd get him in trouble with Margo for sure if he was on his phone after that.

Mandy looped her arm through mine, as if she were determined to see me safely to our seats. According to Stacey, Mandy wasn't convinced the baby hiccups were hiccups. If it were up to her, I'd be on bed rest. Thankfully, Stacey had assured me that Noah was prone to hiccups before he was born, too.

I pulled out my phone and used my thumb to quickly text Hal *What company?*

Hal had caught on to everything I'd done so far. He should realize I was following up on our earlier conversation.

The movie screen lit up. The phone announcement was first

up. If Hal was going to be able to get a message back to me, it was going to be while he was pretending to turn his phone off.

We were only two feet from our seats now. I was going to have to turn my phone off too.

The three dots indicating that he was writing a response appeared. A single word.

Ironclad.

It was the same company that had been robbed in the newspaper articles that Jordan was reading in the *Courier Press* archives.

Her death might have had nothing to do with her job after all.

20

"Why would Jordan have been researching that robbery in the first place?" Mark asked as we helped Nancy pack up the few items from the concession stand that hadn't been eaten. "I think that's your starting point."

Our *Comments* basket was full with the slips of paper we'd provided with questions we wanted people to answer for feedback. Stacey and I would be going over them together next week so we could make adjustments before our official grand opening of Movies in the Woods. The traffic in Fair Haven had already increased this week thanks to tourists, and once school let out, the population of the town would more than double.

Mark snapped the top closed on the last of Nancy's containers. "Most people don't go digging around in cold cases for fun."

Aside from people like Mandy who had an insatiable

curiosity for the unexplained, Mark was right. Jordan didn't have a history of investigating cold cases.

Perhaps her brush with an investigation inside her company had whet her appetite for it. Even so, digging back into a case that was almost as old as she was and had nothing to do with her field of expertise wasn't the logical place to start if she'd decided to become an amateur sleuth. I'd have expected her to start with other potential corruption within the pharmaceutical industry or even falsified scientific studies.

Best guess, she had some kind of personal connection to this case. It was too late to call Zach tonight, even if that would have helped. He hadn't recognized Otto's name. He wasn't likely to suddenly remember a connection between him and his family.

If Hal had time to go with me next week, the easiest thing to do seemed to be to meet with Otto ourselves and ask him.

In the meantime, I had another call to make, regardless of how late it was. Mark and Russ wouldn't let me help pack up anything heavy, which meant I had a half hour or so to kill if I didn't want to walk back home alone in the dark.

It was the right amount of time to call my parents.

"IS SOMEONE DEAD OR DYING?" MY MOM ASKED.

Her voice had that groggy-but-trying-to-pretend-I'm-not tone to it that people had when they answered the phone and didn't want the person on the other end to know they were sound asleep. My mom probably didn't care that I knew she'd been asleep. In fact, her question said she expected I knew and was waking them up for a good reason. But she'd developed that tone of voice in case they got a work call in the middle of the night. I used to wake up in the night and listen to her tone from my bed. In a strange way, it'd been soothing. It'd let me know that everything was normal.

It hadn't been the tone of her voice when they got the call about my Uncle Stan.

My mom was waiting for an answer. I'd been thinking about how to approach this with my parents all through the movie. I'd actually started to appreciate having Hal around, but that didn't excuse them hiring him secretly.

"No one's dead or dying. I wanted to give you a chance to explain why you couldn't have just asked me."

She'd know what I was talking about. There was only one thing I could mean.

She made a *pfft* noise. "When I started dating your dad, your grandfather hired a private investigator to follow him around for a week to vet him. He didn't tell me. It wasn't his job to tell me. It was his job to take care of me. We decided to make sure you and our grandchild were safe. That's our job."

In the past, the insecure voice that hid in my head would have tried to tell me that they felt I needed caring for because I couldn't take care of myself. Because I was lesser and weaker somehow.

I waited again, but the voice didn't come.

Instead, I just had the feeling of being loved. A feeling that my baby was already loved. This was how my parents showed love. It'd taken me a long time to see it.

"You made a good choice with Hal," I said. "He blends in when he needs to, but he can also play a part."

"Maybe we should try to lure him to DC."

She was only partly joking. It wouldn't be the first time my parents had sniped the most talented people away from another job.

Anderson would never forgive me if I cost him his favorite PI firm. "Then who'd be here to watch out for me when I'm on a case?"

"Solid point." The sound of blankets rubbing against each other whispered through the line, as if she were adjusting to sit up in bed. "Was there any other reason you called?"

I almost said *Just to hear your voice because I miss you and I wish you were here to go through this pregnancy with me.* Almost. My parents didn't like anything that bordered on mushy stuff.

I'd keep it practical. "Only to make sure you still give Hal his bonus. You trained me too well not to figure it out."

My mom chuckled. "He'll keep getting his bonus. I won the wager your dad and I had on how long it'd take you to figure it out and then put the pieces together that we'd done it. He said it'd be middle of next week."

From my mom and dad, that timeline was a compliment.

It was on the tip of my tongue to tell her I loved her. Maybe we'd get there some day. I didn't even need a single hand to count the number of times we'd said it to each other. It wasn't what we did.

So instead, I asked what she won from guessing when I'd figure it out.

"The satisfaction of knowing I was right," she said. "Isn't that enough?"

21

_T_he flaw in my parents' plan was that Hal still had other cases to work for Anderson and his firm's other clients. Because we hadn't planned for him to join me on Monday, we couldn't go talk to Otto, and the next few days I'd be in court for jury selection on Zach's case.

I'd almost considered visiting Otto myself, but Mark's "Please don't go alone" plea won me over.

Only a foolish person ignored the counsel of so many people they trusted. If everyone was that worried about me, I needed to listen. And, honestly, I didn't want to put myself unnecessarily in danger. I hadn't intended to end up in so many life-threatening situations in such a short amount of time.

So I'd stay away from Otto Corder until Hal could come with me.

That didn't mean I couldn't call him.

Jordan had been communicating on and off with him for a few weeks. It seemed unlikely she'd do that if she were afraid of him or felt he was a threat. It made more sense that she hoped Otto knew something about the robbery—like who might have committed it. If he'd been working with Ironclad at the time it happened, he could know who'd been dissatisfied with the company, who'd been struggling financially, or even who altered their behavior in the days leading up to the robbery or following it.

Whoever that person was might be the one who really killed Jordan.

Why Jordan felt he'd tell her those things and that she'd be able to figure it out when the police hadn't...that was another question I'd have to deal with afterward. There had to be a link to Jordan that I didn't yet see.

I dialed the number that I'd taken off her phone.

"Hello?" a man's voice said. He had a slight accent, faint enough that it suggested he'd been living in America for most of his life but that he'd been born somewhere that English wasn't his first language.

"Is this Otto Corder?" I asked.

"Yes."

I was used to people sounding leery when I cold-called them. We lived in a world where a lot of people didn't even answer their phones anymore if they didn't recognize the number thanks to all the scam calls and telemarketers.

Otto sounded more curious than suspicious. Almost like he might enjoy toying with telemarketers when they called.

I gave him my name. "I'm following up on the Jordan Williams case. I saw the two of you had exchanged calls."

I stopped and let the implication hang. Most people would fill in how they knew the person or why they'd been calling.

"Hmm," Otto said, "it must have been a wrong number."

My scalp tingled. If the calls had been innocent, why lie about knowing her? It was a big risk to bluff in this situation. He had to think it was his best of bad options or he'd panicked. He didn't sound like he was panicking. Most people who could cover panic that well in their voices also managed to think clearly through it. They wouldn't say something in the heat of the moment that would be difficult to corroborate.

But I'd play along. Blatantly calling him out as a liar would only tip my hand.

"Are you sure?" I added a note of confusion to my voice like the mistake might really be mine. "The paperwork I was given said there were multiple calls back and forth. Jordan Williams. J as in juice. O as in octopus. R as in rain. D as in dog. A as in ant. N as in nut."

He probably thought I was a nut with the words I'd chosen to spell her name out. I knew the NATO phonetic alphabet—my parents required it in their offices when we were spelling out names over the phone—but I wasn't going to use it and give away that I was more than a paper-pusher just doing her job.

"Ah, Jordan. I thought you said Rordan. I don't know a Rordan. Jordan was the daughter of an old co-worker. When I heard he'd passed away, I called a few times to check on her."

Nice try. But the first call came from Jordan to him, not the other way around.

Now still wasn't the time to openly call him out, though. Not until I could find out a bit more. I'd let him think he'd solved everything.

"Thanks!" I added exuberance into my voice this time. "That explains it, and now I don't have to fill out extra paperwork for a wrong call."

"My pleasure," Otto said. "You have a nice day now."

He disconnected the call.

I leaned back on my couch. Toby lifted his head from the floor and whined softly.

"Don't worry, buddy. I'm not going anywhere."

Poor dog. It had to be a stressful job to feel like you had to keep an eye on someone round the clock. When the baby was born, I'd take a picture of him or her with Toby and bring it to Toby's former owner, Bonnie. She'd already been worrying that I wouldn't continue visiting her in prison once the baby was born. I certainly wouldn't take the baby to prison, but I had plenty of people already angling for babysitting privileges. One of them could watch the baby, and I could keep Bonnie updated with pictures.

I put a pillow under my feet. The baby kept me up in the

night with hiccups, so I was more tired than usual. Mark had noticed my restlessness and had joked that, at least once the baby was born, he could help when he or she was fussy in the night.

I shifted as slowly as possible so as not to disturb Toby or my comfortable position and pulled the phone call log from my bag. Jordan had called Otto enough times that it seemed like more than a simple *I think you robbed a bank*. Or, more specifically, *I think you robbed an armored car that belonged to the company you worked for.*

What would there have been left for her to say, after all? Once she had some proof that he was working there at the time —probably even working the day of the robbery if she'd called him so many times—there wouldn't have been any reason for her to keep calling him. Or any reason for him to keep calling her.

But he had lied about knowing her at first. That could be because he was worried I wasn't who I said I was. If he had information that could expose whoever had robbed the armored car, he wouldn't want that person somehow finding out that he knew. It could put his life in danger the way something had Jordan's. He'd certainly realize that.

Which brought me back to the question of how Jordan figured it out. How did she know Otto would be a good source of information about the armored car robbery? Ironclad must have had multiple employees. According to her phone records, she hadn't called anyone else who worked there.

Unless...

I straightened, and Toby flinched in his sleep. Beside him, Velma growled low in her throat even though she didn't open her eyes.

I touched Velma head with my fingertips, and she quieted.

Unless Otto hadn't been completely lying when he said he was an old co-worker of Jordan's father.

One of the unpleasant tasks family had after someone died was sorting through the deceased's belongings—clothes, other personal items, and papers. It'd taken me weeks to get through everything my Uncle Stan left behind.

Jordan might have found something in her father's belongings that pointed to who had committed the robbery. If Jordan had met Otto Corder a couple of times when her father was still alive, he'd have been the natural choice to turn to if she had questions once her father passed away.

And since Jordan had been their father's primary caregiver, Zach likely wouldn't have been around during Otto's visits. Jordan might have even driven her father to visit Otto. Zach didn't live with them, which explained why he hadn't recognized Otto's name on the list.

I needed to talk to Otto Corder in person, when he couldn't hang up and it'd be harder to lie. In person, I could read his body language. But that would have to wait until Hal could join me. Just in case Otto had been involved with the robbery, I wanted backup.

In the meantime, I could call Ironclad Armored Car Services and confirm that Jordan's dad worked there at the same time.

Whatever it was Jordan had uncovered about that armored car robbery might be linked to her death, and Otto was our only chance of finding out what that was.

22

*I*ronclad Armored Car Services was still in business, but the woman who answered the phone said that the names of past employees was something she was sure they couldn't give out without a warrant or a court order or something. She sounded young enough that I asked to speak with a manager. Instead, she put me on hold, presumably spoke to the manager while I was waiting, and came back to tell me that their employee records were private.

I couldn't tell if she'd actually spoken to someone else or not. The company didn't have any other phone number listed, and I'd bet that the email address went to the same receptionist.

Which left me with two options. I could drive to their main office and hope she'd been lying. That carried a huge risk of wasting my time. I might arrive there only to find that she had asked the manager, and I wasn't getting any information from them.

Or I could contact Zach and ask him where his dad worked.

I normally tried to limit how many curiosity-inducing questions I asked clients. My parents had taught me that it was better to corroborate information from an outside source rather than depending on a client to get it right. They also didn't want their clients getting false hope or jumping to any conclusions based on extra questions. They only brought a defense option to a client once it was finished.

I mostly followed their pattern. With Zach, I also tended to get the impression that I was bothering him whenever I needed to meet with him. Unlike most other clients I'd worked with, he didn't even seem to care about regular updates on the progress of his case.

This time, I didn't have a choice about contacting him. I'd text him instead of calling, though. It might not be as fast, but it was less intrusive.

Do you remember where your dad worked when you were a kid? I typed.

I started to set my phone aside, but the three dots that indicated he was writing a response appeared on my screen. I waited.

He worked a lot of places. Why?

The *why* question was exactly what I'd wanted to avoid. Clients tended to get grouchy if you spent time working on a defense strategy that didn't pan out. It was like they thought you were wasting your fee.

They liked it less if they asked you a question and you refused to answer.

I tapped the side of my phone. Maybe he'd let me get away with a polite dodge. *Not sure if it's relevant or not yet. Could you list them for me?*

He drove a semi for a while. Worked security. Can't remember if he worked anywhere else.

Those were related fields to working for an armored car company, but Zach hadn't been able to state for certain that he had worked for Ironclad or even that he worked for an armored car service.

I could send Zach the name Ironclad and see if it sounded familiar, but the thought made me feel squirmy inside. Working with clients I didn't like wasn't abnormal. It wasn't so much that I didn't like Zach as that I just wasn't comfortable communicating with him. Something about him was off-putting. It didn't bode well for him if this went to trial and we needed to put him in front of a jury.

My mom's voice started up in my head about how it didn't matter whether I was comfortable or not, and that a good lawyer would learn to be comfortable in any situation. That it'd be my job to instruct Zach on how to make a jury like him, as well.

The worst part was that her made-up voice was right. Besides, my problem likely had nothing to do with Zach at all and everything to do with being generally tired and spending my days around dogs who were now even more paranoid than I was.

I'd ask Zach more specific questions if I had to. For now, I'd take the chicken way out and ask Hal. He wouldn't be able to look into anything today, but that was okay too. He wasn't free to try to visit more leads until Friday.

I switched over to my text message stream with Hal. *Can you run a background report on Jordan and Zach Williams' father?*

I gathered up the dogs and took them for a walk while I waited for a response. We barely got down the lane before the overcast sky opened up and drenched us. It was for the best, really. I needed a nap more than the dogs needed a long walk.

My phone pinged as I was wiping muddy dog paws before letting them loose in the house again. I finished and checked my phone.

Already did, Hal had written. *What do you need to know? Did he work for Ironclad Armored Car Services?*

I stared at the screen. Finally, the dots showed up and another text came in.

For ten years.

He gave the start and end dates.

He'd left Ironclad a few months after the robbery.

23

Hal and I decided that the best idea was to wait until the day we wanted to visit Otto and ask him last-minute to meet with us. If he was involved in something or knew something, that gave him less time to practice any lies. It also meant he couldn't agree in order to placate us and then cancel on us last-minute.

Since I'd already called and set up the idea that we were following up on Jordan's calls in her last days, we decided I would call Otto again and say we were talking to everyone who had contact with her because we were trying to establish her state of mind. We needed to speak to him in person because we needed a signed statement, otherwise we'd have to subpoena him to appear in court.

Most people, when given the chance, would do almost anything to avoid having to show up in court. There was a reason avoiding jury duty was almost a cultural joke. I'd personally always thought it'd be fun to be on the jury for a change, but as a lawyer, I was automatically disqualified from serving as a juror.

I dialed Otto's number.

"Hello?" a woman's voice said.

Hmm. The number must be for a landline to their house rather than Otto's cell phone. I asked for Otto.

"You missed him." His wife didn't have the same accent as he did. "This is the first nice day for fishing. He headed out as the sun was coming up to Big Bend Island."

If we waited and called back, we'd lose our element of surprise the same as if we'd scheduled a meeting ahead. I gave her the spiel I'd come up with about needing an affidavit.

"Will you need me to sign one too?" the woman asked. "She only visited once. Otto talked to her more on the phone. But I'd still be happy to help. It must be awful for her family not knowing whether she took her own life or someone killed her."

She must not have heard that Zach had been arrested for Jordan's murder.

She'd also already accidentally given me one useful piece of information. Otto and Jordan hadn't only exchanged phone calls. An in-person meeting suggested they felt the need for added secrecy. Or that Jordan—like me—wanted to see his face as she talked to him.

"Was that visit the last time either of you spoke to her?"

"Oh no. That was after the first time she called Otto. Otto always regretted losing touch with her dad after they both left Ironclad."

They hadn't been in touch after they left Ironclad.

What if it wasn't that Jordan and Zach's dad knew something about the armored car robbery? What if it was that he took part in it instead? With Otto.

If he'd been in on the robbery with her father, he might have even followed her home to learn where she lived in order to come back later and kill her. Someone who could plan an armored car robbery that went unsolved for this long could also plan a murder—assuming he'd been the brains behind the heist.

I wished I'd put the call on speakerphone so that Hal could have heard what I did, but people could tell when they were on speaker, and then I'd have had to explain it.

Either way, it didn't sound like Otto's wife knew anything other than the cover story that Otto had fed her. Or she was a good actress, too. She'd worked as a hospital receptionist. She might have still had some connections who could have sourced the SUX that was used on Jordan.

Even if she wasn't directly involved, Otto might have learned about SUX through her time working in a hospital environment.

We'd have to come back to her later. Right now, I wanted to get to Otto before the two of them had a chance to talk. "We might need your statement, too, but I'm supposed to start with your husband. His name is the one on my list."

"You can try to find him at the lake. He usually comes in around noon after the fish stop biting."

"That was Big Bend Island, you said, and he stops fishing at noon?"

I repeated what she'd said for Hal's benefit. He pulled out his phone. He met my gaze and nodded. We could make it there in time to be waiting for Otto when he brought his boat in.

"That's right," his wife said. "Let me give you the license plate number of our truck. That way you can find it in the parking lot and have a better chance of catching him."

If she knew the real way in which I wanted to catch her husband, she likely wouldn't have been nearly as helpful.

OTTO'S TRUCK WAS PARKED IN THE PARKING LOT NEXT TO THE boating docks at Big Bend Island Lake, just as his wife said he would be. My watch said 11:49. We'd barely made it in time after a GPS malfunction took us to a spot on the opposite side of the lake from the boat launch that Otto's wife said he preferred. We'd left my car behind and set out walking, thinking the dock had to be close to the parking lot we'd found. It wasn't, but by the time we realized it, it was quicker to walk to the actual location than it would have been to turn back.

"Now I guess we wait until the owner shows up," Hal said.

"You won't have to wait long," the same slightly accented

voice I'd talked to on the phone said. "Did you bump into the truck or the trailer?"

He'd assumed that the only reason we'd be waiting for him was if we'd damaged his property. It made sense.

He came around the front of the truck and stopped with his arms crossed over his chest.

His voice fit his appearance. He had thick silver hair, heavy eyebrows, and eyes that were almost a teal color. Maybe it was his nose or his jawline, but something about him said he might be of Eastern European descent.

I stepped up beside Hal. "We didn't hit either of them." I extended my hand. "We spoke on the phone earlier this week. I had some follow-up questions, and your wife helped us find you."

Otto shook my hand, brief but firm, like he wasn't shaken up at all by our appearance but like he didn't want to spend much time with us either. "I recognize your voice." He nodded back toward the water, where a boat bobbed, tied to the dock by two ropes. "There's not much more to tell, but if you want me to talk, you can help me with my boat first. It's a lot easier getting it on the trailer with extra hands."

He pointed toward the dock. He must mean for us to wait there while he backed the trailer into the water. My parents' boat was large enough that it stayed in the water all season, and a professional service hauled it out in the winter and stored it until spring. I'd never participated in putting a boat on a trailer, but I'd seen it done a few times.

Mark and I should consider buying a small boat. I'd always loved being out on the water on the rare occasions my parents used our boat, and I'd like our child to have the same experience. Besides, Mark wouldn't get seasick in a small boat where he'd be out in the open air.

I craned my neck to see if there was a brand name of some sort on Otto's boat, the way cars were labeled with Ford or Chevrolet or Audi.

I stumbled on an uneven board on the dock and caught myself on the post Otto had tied the front rope to. The knot was one I'd seen before. Was it because my dad taught me how to tie a few sailor's knots when I was younger? Or was it that this was the same knot used to tie Jordan's noose?

I couldn't remember the knot from the pictures well enough.

If they matched, we'd just found Jordan's killer.

Hal stood at the edge of the dock, directing Otto as he backed up his truck. I needed to snap a picture before they untied the boat, hopefully without Otto catching me at it in case they matched.

I pulled out my phone and tried to make it look like I was sending a text message. With his only view of me being whatever he glimpsed in his rearview mirror, Otto shouldn't know that I was actually taking a picture. At least that was the theory I had to work with.

I couldn't zoom in—the motion on my screen would be too obvious—so I snapped three images in case one wasn't clear enough.

I tucked the phone back into my purse and went to the rear rope to wait. We moved the boat up onto the trailer. Hal and the water did most of the work. Otto waded out into the water and winched the boat up onto the trailer.

Otto climbed back into the truck. He slowly pulled the trailer out of the water, then picked up speed. For a second, I thought he might keep on driving and leave us here.

He slowed down again and pulled the trailer out of the way, under a tree.

He didn't climb back out of his truck. Instead, he rolled down the window and rested an arm on the edge. It was a posture that said he'd honor his agreement to talk to us, but that he wasn't going to give us an indefinite period of time to do it. He wasn't interested in hanging around.

Hal and I had come up with a plan on the drive. Since I'd played "assistant" on the phone, we'd decided that Hal should take the lead this time, and I could chime in as the sweet, bumbling sidekick.

Hal planted a foot on the running board of Otto's truck, a counterpoint to Otto staying inside. Now he wouldn't be able to drive away without knocking Hal over. "What do you know about Hank Williams' involvement with the robbery of the Iron-clad armored car during your time working there?"

The interaction I'd had with Otto on the phone had suggested he had an innate confidence. Hal and I had decided the best way to counter that was to come at this as if we had definitive proof about Williams' part in the crime rather than that we were guessing. We had to go in strong or Otto would brush us off. Even if we turned out to be wrong about Hank Williams' involvement in the crime, he'd wonder what we had that made us think Hank Williams had been involved as long as we came in confident enough.

Otto met Hal's gaze and held it. "I don't know what you're talking about." His words came out deadpan, no inflection, no hesitation, no eye flicker. "So I guess that means I don't know anything about it."

His response was so instinctive that it could mean he was telling the truth, but I still got the impression that he came across that way because he had years of experience lying about it.

He didn't ask the question I'd have expected an innocent man to ask. A guilty man or an innocent man could have asked why we thought he'd know something. An honest man would have asked why we thought Hank Williams had been involved. That question came instinctively to people when they found out someone they knew had been accused of a crime.

Otto didn't ask it, and it gave him away. He knew something about what had happened all those years ago.

Which meant we needed to push and see if we could shake him.

"I have Jordan's notes here somewhere." I fumbled around with my purse as if there should be proof Jordan left behind inside. "He can read them if he wants."

Hal held up a hand toward me in a *stop* motion. I removed my hands from my purse and slumped my shoulders. Hal being able to stop me so completely and my subservient reaction should make Hal come across to Otto as confident and strong—someone Otto shouldn't lie to.

"According to the notebook the police found in Jordan's house," Hal said, "she'd figured out that the robbery that took place during the time you and her father both worked for Iron-clad was an inside job. She had evidence that her father was part of it. She also knew he couldn't have pulled it off alone."

Hal held eye contact with Otto. He hadn't said that we believed Otto was the accomplice. It'd be up to Otto to decide whether that's what Hal was implying. Hal could also be hinting that he thought the accomplice was someone else that Otto was covering for. Otto's guilt or innocence would determine what he read into Hal's statement.

Coming at it that way gave us the advantage. If we were wrong about Otto being involved—though I was now sure we weren't—he might give us the person who actually had been behind it.

Otto kept his gaze steady. "Are you two the police?"

Not one of the responses we'd expected. It also wasn't one we'd planned for. Hal had no badge to pull out, and we wouldn't have tried that even if we had anticipated it. Impersonating an officer was a crime.

Hal simply said, "No. We've been hired to investigate."

It was a good try. He hadn't lied. We were hired to investigate. That gave his words an innate ring of honesty. He'd merely left out the part that the police hadn't been the ones who hired us. If Otto filled that blank in the way Hal obviously hoped, we might still have a chance.

Otto shifted his truck into drive. "Then I think this conversation is over. My wife's expecting me home for lunch, and if you follow me there, I'll consider it trespassing and have to call the real police."

Otto inched the truck forward. Hal wobbled and removed his foot.

The knot might be enough to get the police to look into Otto, but it wasn't likely. They were convinced Zach had killed Jordan. Unique as the knot was, they could still brush it off, saying more than one person in the world would know how to tie it. Unless Otto had invented it, the police would be right.

We had to keep Otto talking to us somehow. I darted forward and placed a hand on my stomach. The bump had grown in the past few weeks. It was still small enough that it could be mistaken for a pudgy belly, but hopefully Otto would recognize it as belonging to a baby. "We parked all the way on the other side of the lake, and it's getting hot out. Would you be willing to at least give us a ride back to our car?"

It wasn't a ploy I would have tried had I been alone. Getting into the car with Otto alone would have been stupid. With two of us, Otto shouldn't try anything. He'd been smart enough to pull off an armored car robbery and possibly smart enough to kill Jordan without leaving an obvious link back to himself. He'd know that to get away with a crime, you needed a well-thought-out plan. If we hopped into his truck with him, he wouldn't have time to come up with one.

Otto's gaze shifted to the road and came slowly back. His hands tightened around the wheel. "The main road's hot and takes twice as long." He pointed behind us, past the building that housed the restrooms. "There's a dirt road that way. If you parked on the other side, that one'll get you there in two-thirds of the time and it's shaded most of the way."

The man was either even smarter than I thought or a real jerk. What kind of person wouldn't give a lift to a pregnant woman?

Otto rolled up his window but didn't drive away.

I got the feeling he was watching to see if we actually took the road he indicated. No doubt he thought we were parked nearby and that I'd been lying to trick him. The joke was on both of us. I had been trying to trick him, but I hadn't been lying.

We walked past the restrooms. The main paved road branched off on the other side, staying paved in the direction that it headed away from the lake and turning into a much narrower gravel road as it stayed close to the lake.

Thankfully, Otto had been telling the truth about how shady the gravel road was. Thick trees lined both sides. It took away the view of the lake, but the temperature dropped by ten degrees as soon as we stepped into the shadows. There wasn't a sidewalk, or even a shoulder, but a speed limit sign said 30 MPH. At the lower speed, we should be easy enough to spot and avoid. We stayed close to the edge regardless. Hal made sure to walk on the inside, putting me farther away from any cars that might pass.

Hal wiped his forehead with the edge of his t-shirt sleeve. "You might have to go to the station that originally investigated the robbery and tell them your suspicions. He's not going to talk to us anymore."

Hal's idea was probably the best solution I was going to get at this point. The officers who investigated Jordan's murder weren't going to re-open the case when I didn't have anything better to offer them than a rope knot that I wasn't even sure matched yet. The department who originally handled the armored car robbery might be willing to take a look again on less, especially if I told them it could be related to a current murder.

The leaves above us shifted in a breeze, and the sunlight that came in reflected off of something at the side of the road. I shaded my eyes. A teenage girl sat cross-legged in the grass along the edge, a bike lying beside her. She had what looked like a sock pressed to her knee.

"Are you okay?" I called out.

She made a face. "My tire blew out, and I scraped up my knee." She held up her phone. "My dad should be here any second."

It might be true. It might not. It was the kind of story I would have told strangers if I was out here alone. Claiming that her dad would be there soon gave a layer of security. Someone with ill intentions might reconsider if they thought they could be caught by her arriving father.

"Thanks for checking, though," she said. "Two cars drove by since I've been here and either ignored me or didn't see me."

I wouldn't have seen her if the light hadn't hit the reflector on her bike just right. Her bike was green and so was her shirt. Combined with her black bike helmet and dark blue shorts, she blended right into the scenery.

Hopefully someone was coming for her. We should probably drive back this way, even though it was in the opposite direction, to make sure she wasn't still sitting here alone.

She didn't make eye contact with us as we passed by.

The sound of a vehicle moving faster than speed limit behind us reached my ears. That was likely whoever she'd called now. I'd have driven faster than I should have too if my daughter had called to say she was sitting in a ditch bleeding. That's how Stacey would have phrased it in that teenage way of sometimes being unaware of how things might sound to others.

My phone buzzed. I paused and reached for it.

Someone screamed—a high-pitched girl's voice—and a blow hit my shoulder.

I stumbled sideways. My feet tangled over each other, and I pitched through the air.

The baby! my mind screamed.

I couldn't land on my belly.

I threw out my arms and twisted, grabbing for anything I could reach, hoping I could at least land in a way that would better protect the baby.

My nails scraped against bark, and I latched on. Strain rammed through my wrists, elbows, and shoulders. My momentum slowed. A snapping noise, and my knees connected with the ground no harder than if I'd lost my balance while kneeling down.

Tires squealed away with the sound of spitting gravel.

I stared down at my hands and the wood still in them. It wasn't so much a branch as a small tree that now was half a tree.

What had happened? It felt like someone pushed me. Why would someone push me?

I dropped the branch and crawled back around to face the road.

Two people were in the middle. One lying down and one sitting beside them. My mind struggled to process it.

The sitting figure turned back toward me. The teenage girl who'd been by the side of the road. "He's bleeding. I don't know what to do."

24

My mind snapped back into place like I'd been fighting to unlock a door that wouldn't give and the key finally slid into position.

Someone tried to run us down. Hal pushed me out of the way. He hadn't been able to get out of the way himself.

I scrambled to my feet and sprinted to their side.

"Call 911," I told the girl.

She nodded and dialed, but then she turned around and gagged.

My face felt unnaturally hot and bile burned the bottom of my throat—only partly from the girl's sound effects. I'd probably be doing the same thing if I'd had someone else to take over. But I couldn't now. She shouldn't have even been involved with this, and Hal needed help.

Blood smeared the side of Hal's face and darkened the ground under his head. His eyes were open.

I sat on the ground next to him and put my hand over his. "Don't move. Help's coming."

Thankfully, it wasn't a lie. The girl was wiping her mouth and talking to someone on the phone.

Hal moved his lips. It might have been a smile that he didn't have the strength to complete. "I know." His voice sounded frayed around the edges. "I didn't see the driver, but it was a black truck."

Like Otto's.

Hal didn't have to say it. It was too much of a coincidence for me not to catch on.

Would he have been that bold? He had directed us to a road that he thought would be mostly deserted. If he had been the one, he probably hadn't seen the girl sitting in the grass by the side of the road.

"I got a photo." The girl spun back toward us. Her gaze shifted. "No, I won't hang up. I'll put you on speaker."

She tapped her screen, presumably switching the 911 operator over to speaker phone and then tapped a few more times. "He hit me with a stone"—she turned her forearm toward me, revealing a red welt—"so I thought if I was quick enough I could...my dad works for the mayor's office and I thought maybe..."

Whatever she thought her dad could do about it originally,

her photo was now evidence in a hit and run, possibly an attempted murder.

Dear God, let it only be an *attempted* murder.

Hal was still breathing and holding onto my hand even though his eyes were pinched shut. That they were pinched told me he was still conscious.

"Take deep, slow breaths," I said.

"That's what they told my wife the times she was in labor." Hal's eyes fluttered open, then closed again. "She said it didn't help."

The girl flipped her phone so the screen faced me. The picture was off center and a little blurry. She'd reacted quick to even be able to get a picture at all. I was already out of the shot, so this was almost at the same time as the truck hit Hal.

"Can you zoom in on his license plate?" I asked.

The image might be too blurry once she did, but we had to try. We had zero proof otherwise that it'd been Otto. If he'd taken this risk, he surely had a plan for how to cover his tracks.

The girl made the pinch-glide motion on her screen. "I think it's..." She squinted and read the letters and numbers.

I didn't need the police to run the plates to confirm my suspicion. I knew that license plate number. Otto's wife had given it to me less than two hours ago. "The man in the truck was Otto Corder."

I rattled off his address.

Sirens wailed softly in the distance, growing louder. I leaned a little closer to Hal. "They're here. You're going to be okay."

"Just don't—" He groaned. "Don't tell my wife what happened. She made me quit the military because she was afraid I'd get myself killed."

"I think it's going to be a little hard to hide it from her." I tried to keep my voice light. "Once you're back on your feet, she's going to want the whole story."

His hand went limp in mine.

I squeezed it. "Hal?"

No response.

25

The EMTs let me ride in the ambulance with Hal once the girl—whose name I learned was Cora because she started spouting her personal information as soon as the police cars rolled up—told them I'd almost been run down, too.

Somewhere on the ride to the hospital, Hal's pulse turned thready, and I stopped thinking about Otto and started praying. Hard.

I called Anderson and got Hal's home phone number. Margo needed to know what was going on long before the hospital or police would be able to contact her. It was what I'd want if the roles were reversed and Mark was close to coding in an ambulance. I'd want my best possible chance to make it to the hospital.

Margo answered, and I skipped the *hello* and went straight

to *There's been an accident*. I explained as quickly as I could what had happened.

Margo cursed. "I tried to tell him there were other ways to help people. That he didn't need to be a human meat shield to be of service." She let out a breath that sounded like it was the last line of defense between her and tears. "I'm coming. Please stay on the phone with me. I want to know what's happening. What they're doing to him."

That didn't sound like the safest way to drive, but I wasn't going to argue with her. If I didn't give her the play-by-play, she'd only drive more recklessly to get here sooner.

Two women and a man, all wearing scrubs, met us at the emergency room doors and swarmed the gurney the EMTs had put Hal on. They rolled him inside.

Hal convulsed on the stretcher.

"His throat's swelling shut," one of the female staff members said. From the way the others deferred to her, I would have guessed she was the doctor and they were the nurses. "We need to get him intubated."

It wasn't like on the medical shows on TV. There wasn't yelling or running. It all felt like a play where everyone had practiced their parts and knew exactly what role they needed to fill.

Everyone except me. And Margo.

I repeated to her everything that was going on.

One of the nurses drew liquid into a syringe from a vial and dropped the not-quite-empty vial into the pocket of her scrubs. She injected the fluid into Hal's leg. He stopped moving.

Was that what it was supposed to do? Or was this a new complication?

I told Margo. I was beginning to feel like a sportscaster at the world's most awful event.

"What are they giving him?" Margo said.

A horned blared in the background on her end, and I flinched. Hopefully she paid enough attention to her driving to not get into a wreck. Their kids didn't need both parents in the hospital—or worse.

"He's allergic to penicillin," she said. "Make sure they know."

I moved in as close as I could without getting in the way. "His wife wants to know what you're giving him. He's allergic to penicillin."

"We found the dog tag with his allergy," the nurse said. "We're giving him succinylcholine so we can get a breathing tube into him."

Earlier on in this case, I'd wanted to know how SUX worked. Now I was getting a close-up look.

Hal lay limp on the gurney. The nurses went to work inserting a breathing tube. I looked away and met the lady doctor's gaze.

"You shouldn't be here." The doctor shot a where's-her-babysitter glare at me. "We don't have time for twenty questions."

"She needs to be examined, too," a familiar man's voice said from behind me. "She's pregnant, and the EMTs said she fell during the hit-and-run."

I whirled around.

Zach stood nearby. He wore the same scrubs, and the same tired expression, he'd had the day we first met. "Let's get you checked in and into a bed."

I told Margo they weren't going to let me stay with Hal anymore.

"I'm pulling up anyway," she said.

At least with her here, Hal would have someone who could advocate for him. It also meant they'd give her updates. Without her here, they wouldn't tell me anything about his condition as things progressed. I wasn't even family.

Zach helped me up onto a bed and handed me a clipboard with paperwork on it. "What happened?"

My eyes struggled to focus on the papers. I shifted my gaze back to where I'd last seen Hal. They'd taken him away into a private room. "We were investigating a lead in Jordan's murder. You remember the name Otto Corder from the list of phone numbers?"

Zach nodded.

"We think he and your father robbed an armored car together, and Jordan found out. He might have killed her because she wanted to expose him."

That part still didn't line up. If Jordan had planned to expose

Otto, why not do it rather than calling him? But it was the best theory we had at the moment, and Otto had tried to kill us for asking questions.

"My dad might have known Otto stole money, and he might have told Jordan about it before he died, but I can't believe he was involved." Zach handed me a hospital gown. "You probably don't have long before the police show up to question you, so you might want to change quickly."

Zach pulled the curtain around my bed.

I set the paperwork aside and slid into the gown. I tied the lower two ties, providing me modesty on my lower half, but I couldn't reach the upper one. As much as I'd like to blame the baby, I'd never been very flexible.

I crawled back up onto the bed and continued with the paperwork, but the gown kept slipping off my shoulders. Finishing the paperwork took twice as long. Between worrying about Hal, wondering if the police caught Otto, and fussing about the gown slipping too low when I wasn't paying attention, I couldn't concentrate.

"Nicole," Zach said from the other side of the curtain, "the police have some questions for you before the doctor sees you. Are you ready for them to come in?"

I was technically decent, but I wasn't going to be able to focus with the gown the way it was. Zach was my client, but he was also a nurse. He was the best option I had for help at present. Anderson promised to call Mark for me, but at best, Mark would

still be a few minutes out. I'd made Anderson promise to have
him swing by the office and grab a copy of the case files before
he came. I wanted to check the knots as soon as possible so I
could tell the police if they matched. I'd hoped the police would
be a bit slower about questioning me.

"Could you come in first?" I said to Zach. "I need a hand with
something."

Zach ducked through the crack between the curtains.

I held the top of the gown up with one hand and pointed
toward my back with the other. Heat crept up my cheeks. My
back wasn't exactly a private place, but it still felt weird. "I
couldn't finish."

Zach gave one of the first smiles I'd ever seen from him. It
felt trained—like it was the one he practiced for patients to make
them feel more comfortable. If that was the case, it worked. The
flames that felt like they were nipping at my cheeks died down.

Zach knotted the top tie securely. "Guaranteed not to slip,"
he said.

He let the two officers in, a man and a woman. I went
through everything I could remember.

It wasn't much. I hadn't seen Hal get hit. I hadn't seen the
driver of the vehicle. I hadn't even seen the vehicle except in
Cora's pictures.

God was looking out for us by having Cora there. The police
should easily be able to arrest Otto based on her statement and
that picture.

Mark arrived as they were finishing up. He laid a hand on the brown oversized envelop tucked under his arm and raised his eyebrows at me as if to say *You really needed this now?*

He'd understand once I told him why.

Both officers glanced up.

Officer Kincaid—the younger of the two—did a double-take. He shot to his feet and extended his hand to Mark. "You're Dr. Cavanaugh. I attended both your sessions at the forensics conference in Portland last year. I'm hoping to move into homicide one day."

His voice had the same breathy quality that most people got when talking to a movie star. It was too bad my mom wasn't here to see it. She'd have loved it.

Mark had his feet and hips angled toward me like he wanted to make sure I was alright, but he smiled at the man anyway. He pulled a business card out of his pocket. "You can give me a call anytime if you have questions."

The officer accepted the card in a way that reminded me again of a normal person accepting the autograph of a famous athlete.

The older female officer slid a glance in my direction and covered her mouth with her hand like she was trying to hide a smile. Like she knew that, given they were investigating a hit-and-run, she shouldn't be trying not to laugh right now, but she couldn't quite help it.

Officer Kincaid looked at me as well, and his smile fell off his face, turning his lips down. The matching last name must have finally registered, and he was wondering if Mark was thinking he'd never make it as a homicide detective if he missing something obvious like that. Or that he was callous and self-absorbed because he was telling Mark about himself when his wife was lying in a hospital bed.

Knowing Mark the way I did, he wasn't thinking either of those things. He loved it when anyone showed an interest in forensic pathology.

The female officer rose to her feet. "Thank you for your help, Mrs. Cavanaugh. We'll be in touch if we have any more questions."

Officer Kincaid mumbled an additional thanks to Mark and slinked out of the curtained area after her. If he'd been a puppy, his tail would have been between his legs.

Mark sank heavily into the chair vacated by the female officer. "Are you sure you're alright? Anderson said you were, but he hadn't seen you, and neither has a doctor."

"Thanks to Hal, I don't have anything worse than a splinter."

I filled him in on what I knew of Hal's condition, then made a *gimme gimme* gesture with my hands toward the file.

Mark passed it over. "Want to tell me what's going on and why this file was more important than me getting here quickly?"

I pulled the photocopies out of the envelope and flipped through them. "Jordan was hung with a weird knot. I saw another weird knot when we were talking to Otto. I'm hoping they match."

If they did, it could also be another reason Otto tried to run us down. He might have seen me taking the pictures and realized what I was doing.

I handed Mark half the papers. We could find it faster working together, and I wanted to check for a match before the doctor came to examine me.

Mark turned a sheet of paper to face me. "Found it."

I grabbed my phone and tapped through to my camera. The first photo I'd taken was too blurry. I swiped to the second one. Perfect.

I enlarged it and looked back and forth between it and the picture Mark held.

My heart felt like it dipped down in my chest and rested close to where the baby sat.

They didn't match. There was enough of a similarity that they could easily be mistaken for each other if you weren't holding them side by side, but once you did, the differences stood out.

Mark raised his eyebrows, and I shook my head.

I might have gotten Hal hurt for nothing.

No, not entirely for nothing. We might not have Otto for Jordan's murder yet, but we must have been right about his role in the old armored car robbery. He wouldn't have run us down otherwise.

And he could still be the person who murdered Jordan, even though these knots didn't match. He knew about knots. He might have chosen a different one for that situation.

If that were the case, it was going to come down to either getting him to confess or finding another knot we could prove he'd tied that matched. Without the confession, I'd be able to cast reasonable doubt during Zach's trial, but the police wouldn't likely pursue Otto instead of Zach for her murder.

I ran through it all again with Mark while we waited for the doctor. The only thing we came up with were more questions. Like where was the money if Otto Corder and Hank Williams had robbed the armored car? Both of them had appeared to live average lives, and Zach hadn't mentioned a large sum of money that they discovered once his father passed away.

The police suspected Zach killed Jordan in part because of their inheritance. She'd gotten the house, and he hadn't gotten any sort of equal monetary compensation. There hadn't been any large sums of money left over to inherit. What their father had left had only finished paying off the house and his medical bills.

Even with the strokes their father suffered in his final year of life, there should have been money left over. The amount stolen from the armored car would have easily covered his medical expenses and then some. Besides, wouldn't Hank Williams have paid his mortgage off long ago if he'd had that kind of money?

And surely the police would have asked the banks to flag any unusually large deposits either men made in the year, or even years, following the robbery.

The money was off the grid.

The curtain swished aside before we could start building any theories. I looked up expecting to see the doctor.

Zach pulled the curtains closed again instead, as if they could block out sound rather than just sight. "I'm headed home for the day, but first I have good news and bad news."

26

I'd always hated when people started a conversation that way. The only way they could possibly make it worse was when they asked which I wanted first.

My answer was neither. I wanted you to get to the point rather than torturing me with suspense. Saying you had good news and bad news ranked right up there for me with trying to surprise me.

Zach didn't come any further into my curtain cubicle. He stayed with one hand on the curtain he'd closed. "I checked in with your friend's wife. She gave me permission to update you on him."

I grabbed Mark's hand. Was that the good news or the bad news?

"He has a fractured tibia, which they say could have been

much worse given the nature of the accident. They think he must have been clipped rather than hit directly."

That made sense. He'd have pushed me out of the way and then tried to get out of the way himself. He may have even jumped. While I hadn't tested it and hoped not to, I'd heard that if you were going to be hit by a car, you should jump. Your legs would take the brunt of the blow then, rather than your core, where all your internal organs lived.

My heart did a weird kicking beat against the front of my chest. Saying Hal had a fractured tibia sounded like the good news.

"What else?" My voice squeaked slightly. Why did Zach have to be the kind of person with an impassive face that was almost impossible to read?

"They also found a small bleed in his brain. But because they found it so quickly and got him into surgery right away, they're optimistic about the outcome."

From the way Zach almost smiled, I took it that was actually the good news. Anything other than a full recovery in Hal's case wouldn't be good news.

"All we can do now is wait and pray," Mark said.

A doctor parted the curtain for my exam, and Zach left.

Exam might have been a generous term. It turned out he wasn't going to run any tests, so I'd gotten into the thin, drafty hospital gown for nothing. He basically asked me questions about whether I'd felt any pain in my abdomen since the fall or if I was having bleeding. The answer to both questions was *no*.

He was questioning me about my neck and back when Mark's phone rang.

Mark glanced down at the screen, frowned, and answered with. "This is Cavanaugh."

My hands tingled like they'd fallen asleep. *Don't let it be bad news about Hal*, I prayed.

I gave myself a mental shake. Margo wouldn't have called Mark's phone. She didn't even have Mark's number. She'd have called or texted me, or more likely, forgotten all about me if Hal didn't make it through his surgery.

Mark was probably being called in to a crime scene. Thankfully, my "examination" was almost over.

The doctor told me to come back or call my family doctor if anything changed and that I could leave. I should have sat with Margo so she wasn't alone rather than waiting around for what amounted to a pat on the head. My watch said I'd been here for hours already.

Mark asked the person on the phone to wait a second and shook hands with the doctor. The doctor left.

"Are you getting called in?" I asked.

Mark shook his head. "It's Officer Kincaid, from earlier."

That explained why Mark had frowned at the phone. The number would have shown up as a police department, but it wasn't one he worked with because it was in a different county.

"Does he have another question for me?" If that were the case, he could have called me directly. I'd given them my phone number. Though perhaps he'd simply wanted another chance to talk to his hero.

"He called as a professional courtesy to let us know that they caught Otto Corder." Mark passed the phone to me. "I can't put it on speakerphone in a public place, and I thought you'd want to hear the whole story from him."

Darn right I did. I accepted the phone. "I hear you have good news for me." Real good news this time, not *it could have been worse* news like Zach had brought where I wasn't sure what to consider the good news and what to consider the bad.

"Yes, ma'am. It's a good thing you were able to identify Corder's vehicle from the photo the other witness took. Had we been even ten minutes later, we wouldn't have been able to prove he'd faked the theft of his vehicle."

I knew Otto wouldn't have tried to run us down without a plan, but Kincaid skipped a few steps. "Can you back up and start from the beginning? My husband didn't tell me anything except that you found Corder."

"My apologies, ma'am." Kincaid sounded so sincere that I was almost convinced he wasn't being extra nice to me just because I was Mark's wife. "We dispatched officers to Corder's residence, thinking he'd return there, but before they could arrive, we got another call. A bystander called 911, reporting vandalism of a vehicle in the parking lot of Big Bend Island Lake boat dock. The dispatcher asked for a description of the vandal and the license plate on the vehicle. As soon as she entered it in the system, she got a notification for the BOLO—be on the lookout—we'd put out for Corder and his truck."

So that's how Otto planned to get away with it. He'd taken his truck back to the boat dock. He'd probably planned to put his boat back into the water, smash his own window, and then claim he'd been out fishing the whole time when the police came looking for him.

He'd had to do his best at picking a moment when he thought no one was around, but he hadn't been able to wait long. Had he waited too long, the police would have showed up before he could get back out onto the water. He must not have spotted the bystander who called in the vandalism.

Had he succeeded in breaking his window without being spotted, his plan might have worked. We didn't have a picture of the driver, only of the vehicle. I hadn't seen the driver. Cora hadn't been paying attention until the truck threw a stone at her, so she likely hadn't seen the driver. We had no way of knowing yet if Hal could have identified Otto as the driver or not.

Cora being there had helped us in more ways than one. Had she not made her presence known after Otto ran Hal down, he might have turned back to finish me off.

"The police had to bring Corder in off the water," I said aloud, just to confirm I'd put the pieces together correctly.

"How did you know?"

"It made sense that the only reason he would have for breaking his own window was to provide an alibi. He could claim someone stole his truck while he was fishing."

Kincaid made a whistling noise. "Do you work for the police alongside Dr. Cavanaugh?"

"I'm a lawyer, but we've worked together before." Before Kincaid got lost down a rabbit trail of wanting to know more about our work, I should redirect him back to the case. I wanted to get dressed and go find out if there was any fresh news on Hal. And I wanted to be able to tell Margo that I had good news for her about the man who hurt him. "Has Corder been officially arrested?"

Instead of answering, Kincaid went silent. The rise and fall of voices in the background came across his end of the line.

My question had hit some sort of nerve. He didn't want to answer because he didn't want to upset me.

Or because he felt he shouldn't.

"Mark and I both understand the importance of confidentiality, but I'd appreciate whatever information you feel comfortable sharing. My employee—my friend—is still in surgery for bleeding on his brain. Would it be completely impossible for you to tell us anything more?"

"No," Kincaid said. "I suppose not. It won't be an open investigation for much longer anyway. Corder and his lawyer are already talking to the DA about a deal."

Holy crap. I hadn't seen that coming, but it made sense. Otto

Corder was smart. If he'd come to a place where he could either confess and get a reduced sentence or take his chances in court against eyewitnesses and photographic evidence, he'd take a deal.

Mark raised his eyebrows at me in a what's-up? look. I mouthed the words *Otto's confessing*.

Mark's eyebrows went even higher. He moved onto the bed beside me, and I tilted the phone so that we could both listen.

I had a fluttery feeling in my chest, like bubbles were trapped there. This might all be over. Hal would have the peace of mind of knowing that Otto was in prison. "Has he confessed to everything?"

"All of it." Kincaid's voice kipped up as if he would have loved to bounce in his seat like an eight-year-old boy. "The hit-and-run and the armored car robbery. I don't think he was going to confess to that second one, but he talked to his wife and whatever she said must have convinced him."

Otto Corder must have a wife with a conscience. She'd wanted her husband to do the right thing. Who knew what would have happened had she not?

I inched closer to Mark to make sure he could hear clearly. "We suspected he'd been involved with the armored car robbery, but we didn't have any concrete evidence."

"The detective who interrogated him faked that you did. I told him what you said about having claimed his accomplice's daughter left a journal with proof."

Mark squeezed my leg, and I leaned in and quickly brushed

my lips against his. Thank goodness we'd been right about Otto Corder's involvement. Hal wasn't injured for nothing.

"Corder said his accomplice regretted what they'd done almost as soon as they'd done it," Kincaid said, "but it was too late. His partner felt too guilty to use the money, and they were both too scared to turn it in."

Admitting he'd been the one who wanted to use the money gave Otto's story added validity. Had Otto been lying, he would have said Hank Williams was the one who wanted to use the money and he was the one who didn't. Or he'd have at least pretended they'd been in agreement.

The voices in the background on Kincaid's end grew louder, like the owners were walking past. They faded off again.

"They decided the accomplice would hide the money," Kincaid said, "and they'd never speak of it to anyone again."

Either Hank Williams had gone back on that promise and he told Jordan before he died—maybe wanting her to turn the money in once he was gone—or my first guess was right. She'd found something in his personal items after his death that clued her in.

We might never know exactly how Jordan figured it out. She obviously hadn't told Zach that their father was a criminal or Zach would have pointed me in Otto's direction from the start the way he had the whistleblowing situation at Papyrus Medical. He'd told me he couldn't believe their father would do anything criminal. I'd have the unpleasant job of letting him know he'd been wrong.

At least I could soften the blow by also giving him closure about Jordan's death. "Did the detective get details on how Corder killed Jordan Williams?"

"He didn't."

I swallowed down a sigh. I didn't actually need details. My curiosity just wanted them. Zach probably wouldn't ask for them, if I was being honest with myself. He'd only care that he wouldn't have to go to prison for his sister's murder. "I guess we can live with holes as long as Otto confessed and gave enough detail that they're sure he did it."

"Oh, umm," Kincaid's voice took on a squirming-in-his-seat tone, "no, I meant he didn't kill Jordan Williams. He confessed to the hit-and-run and armored car robbery, but he said that he and Jordan had an agreement. She called and confronted him. She wanted him to turn himself in. He told her he wanted the same freedom to live out his life in peace the way her father had. According to him, she felt bad for him, and they agreed that she'd go to the police with what she knew after he died. He was with his wife at the time of Jordan Williams' death."

I leaned against Mark. Mrs. Corder could be lying, but what was the point? Otto was already going to prison for a very long time. He could have bundled Jordan's death into whatever deal he was making. He had no reason to lie about it, and his wife had no reason to alibi him out, especially if she'd convinced him to confess to the robbery.

I thanked Kincaid for his help and passed the phone back to Mark. He ended the call.

An unpleasant weight filled the bottom of my stomach. Dexter Ruffalo hadn't killed Jordan. Otto Corder hadn't killed Jordan.

Kincaid had said the accomplice—Hank Williams—hid the money. The money was still missing. Jordan had found something that had sent her to the newspaper archives to read everything she could find on the robbery. Whatever she found sent her to Otto Corder to try to convince him to turn himself in rather than having the police turn up at his door after she followed through on whatever she'd found.

Otto didn't have the money. Jordan would have kept a hold of the money with the intent of turning it in after Otto passed away.

Jordan seemed like a person who made sure all contingencies were covered. Otto Corder could live for years. She must have known that something could have happened to her before he died, and then someone else would have needed to return the money. She didn't seem like the kind of person who would have been alright with the money simply staying missing should she die before she could turn it in.

She must have had a backup plan. A backup person.

And the most likely candidate seemed to be the brother she

spoke to multiple times a week. The brother she'd thought highly enough of that she'd set him up on a date with her close friend. The brother who should have felt an equal responsibility to make right the wrong their father had committed.

What if I'd been wrong all along? The motive of Jordan inheriting the house instead of him had always seemed like too weak a motivator for Zach to kill his sister. They'd been close.

The money from the armored car robbery, though, was significantly more. Enough that Zach wouldn't have to work again if he invested wisely. He would be able to pay off the student loans he still carried. He wouldn't have to give his ex-wife any of it in alimony because there'd be no official record of it.

He could afford the best law firm in the state.

The memory of the nurse pocketing the part vial of SUX after it'd been used to help intubate Hal filled my mind and pushed every other thought aside.

Otto Corder—or most other people for that matter—wouldn't have had access to SUX. Even if Otto knew about it, even if his wife helped him, they wouldn't have been able to walk into a hospital and pocket a vial. Medication of that potency and danger stayed locked up until it was needed. Otto Corder was too smart to have taken the risk of having his wife ask an old colleague to steal any for them.

But Zach could have dropped a partially used vial into his

pocket the way the nurse had today. Everyone would have assumed he later disposed of it in the proper manner.

I looked up at Mark. "I think I made a mistake."

He reached my side in one stride and grabbed up my wrist. His fingers touched the spot where he could take my pulse. "Are you having pain now? We haven't checked you out yet. They can still send you for tests without waiting."

"It's not that." I twisted the hand he held around so I could link my fingers with his. If I was right...if I was right, I didn't even want to think about what it meant. "How much SUX would it have taken to paralyze Jordan?"

"Not much." His eyebrows came down in the center, and if it was possible, he looked more concerned than he had a second before. "Why?"

"Would someone have been able to pull enough together from what was leftover in a vial or two?"

"Yes." The way he drew out the word sounded like he was suspicious of where I was going with this. And he didn't like the idea any more than I did.

I pulled the picture of the knot used in Jordan's noose back out of the envelop and handed it to Mark. "I need you to check the top knot on my gown. Zach tied it, and he said it was guaranteed not to slip."

27

I slowly turned my back to Mark and sat cross-legged on the hospital bed. Should I hope that I was wrong? Then I'd have to continue the hunt for a killer without any leads.

Or should I hope that I was right? And then I was defending a guilty man. Hal had been injured trying to prove a guilty man innocent.

Mark was quiet long enough that I started to count in my head.

Finally, I couldn't stand it anymore. "You're killing me, Smalls."

"I know what I think, but I want you to see it too. Hand me your phone."

I passed it back over my shoulder, and he handed me the picture of Jordan's noose in return.

My phone made the snapshot sound that mimicked a traditional camera's noise. Mark came around to my front and gave me the phone as well.

It wasn't as easy to tell as it had been with the picture I'd taken of Otto Corder's boat knot. The materials were different—rope vs cloth strings.

Even so, the loops were the same, and one string hung through the other. If I'd wanted to, I could have easily tightened or loosened the gown without risking the knot coming undone. It was perfect for a hospital gown, and it was perfect for a hangman's noose.

I couldn't look at it anymore. I hit the Home button on my phone. "They're the same."

Mark nodded, as if he didn't want to say the words out loud. He knew what this meant to me. The odds were good that I was defending a guilty man. I'd gone back to the place I promised myself I'd never be unless it was to represent someone who wanted to confess, the way Toby's first owner had.

"What are you going to do?" Mark asked.

I was going to call Zach and tell him he needed to be honest with me about what happened to Jordan—whether he was involved or not. I was going to lay out the evidence, tell him what I suspected, and see what he said.

But I was going to do all that tomorrow. Tonight, all I was going to do was whatever Margo needed. For all we knew, she was sitting there alone, waiting for someone to come tell her whether Hal was alive or dead. Her family lived out of state. His might as well.

No one should have to face what she was facing alone.

Zach hadn't wanted to meet with me the next day. I told him it wasn't optional. The outcome of his case was in jeopardy.

As soon as we'd settled into my office, I laid out my suspicions about what really happened to Jordan and why.

Part of me hoped he'd try to defend himself. Or that he'd have some reasonable explanation for why he looked so guilty—one that would assure me of his innocence.

He didn't do any of that. He sat quietly through my whole presentation.

And then he smiled the first real smile I'd seen from him.

"I'm sorry I ever doubted your abilities. I didn't think anyone would figure out the truth, but you did." He leaned onto the arm of his chair, his posture relaxed. "Since you're my lawyer, I suppose there's no reason I can't tell you the truth. You have to keep it confidential. You just seemed so determined to prove I was innocent, I thought it was kinder to let you believe it was true."

My stomach cramped, and heat burned the back of my throat in a way that was much worse than morning sickness because the cause wasn't physical.

He really had lied to me. He really had killed his sister.

As soon as he left, I was going to speak with Anderson and petition the court to be removed as Zach's lawyer. Knowing that he'd lied, Anderson wasn't going to want to represent him, either.

Anderson had modeled his whole practice on my parents' business. That included the cardinal rule. Clients could lie to their family. They could even lie to the police. They couldn't lie to their lawyer because you defended an innocent person differently than you did a guilty one.

Anderson would have explained that to Zach. Zach must have felt he knew better.

The sooner we extricated him from our practice, the better.

My lips wanted to curl at him. I clamped my teeth together so hard that a muscle jumped in my cheek, and I took a couple of breaths through my nose to calm down.

"Then why don't you tell me the truth this time?" I said. "I'd like to hear it from you even though I think I've mostly figured it out."

He bobbed his head. "From the sounds of it, you did. I'm sorry all your work had to be for nothing."

That's what he decided to apologize for? The extra work I'd put in?

My fingers tensed. Deep down inside me there was a desire to actually hit him. It wasn't something I was proud of. I didn't believe that an individual had the right to harm another individual. But I wanted to hit him. Hard.

"You'll be charged for the time wasted, so it's of no concern to the firm." I couldn't quite keep the snideness from my voice. "But please save me the time of having to figure out for myself anything else you should have told me from the start."

Zach's face seemed to harden around the edges. "I didn't actually lie to you. I never said I didn't kill Jordan, not even when you asked."

That was true. He hadn't. He'd said something about Jordan doing it to herself. In hindsight, I could see how he might think that wasn't a lie, even if it had been dodging the actual question. He believed that Jordan brought this on herself because she wouldn't keep the money.

"When did you and Jordan find out that your dad was involved with the Ironclad Armored Car Service robbery?"

Zach's face had gone back to the blank mask that seemed to be his default. I clearly wouldn't be able to tell if he were telling me the truth or not. I hadn't been able to spot his dodges earlier.

But he had no reason to lie to me now. He was right. As his lawyer, there was nothing I could do about his lies.

Except recuse myself from the case the way I planned to do. Few people realized that lawyers needed to be as unbiased as jurors when they were defending a guilty client. If they felt disgust or distaste for their client and they weren't able to hide it, it'd bleed through.

I'd proven that I couldn't adequately defend a guilty client.

Zach didn't smile again, and I was grateful for that. If he'd seemed in the least bit cocky, I might have told him what I thought of him.

"We were clearing out his belongings after he died." Zach's gaze shifted, so that he was looking beside me rather than looking me in the eye. Like he didn't want me to see any emotion that might show up there. "He'd kept a ton of old stuff in the attic that Jordan wanted to pull out and donate to Goodwill before mice got into it. We found the bag of money stuffed behind some insulation in the attic rafters. There was a newspaper clipping from the *Courier Press* about an armored car robbery inside."

I'd been right that Jordan had found something while she was clearing out her dad's things. What I hadn't counted on was that Zach had been helping her. I'd assumed she'd been doing the task alone. That was probably my own bias showing through, since I'd sorted through what my Uncle Stan left behind by myself.

I'd let my own bias influence a lot of what happened in this case. Because Zach had been kind to me when I'd been scared, I'd assumed he cared about all human life and wasn't the kind of person who would murder a family member over money.

I just wanted this to be over with.

"So Jordan went to the *Courier Press* archives to see if she could find out anything more about the robbery and how it connected to your dad." I phrased it as a statement rather than a question. Jordan's actions seemed self-explanatory now.

Zach's eyebrows twitched in a way that made me think he wanted to roll his eyes at what he considered silliness, but he wouldn't give that much away. "I told her it didn't matter where the money came from. We hadn't had anything to do with it."

I knew that Jordan must have insisted on turning the money in. But given how Zach had sidestepped the truth so many times, I needed to say it out loud. "Once she was convinced that your dad stole the money, Jordan wanted to turn the money in to the police, and that's why you killed her?"

Zach nodded. Casually. Like I'd asked him if he had a sandwich for lunch. "Dad had that money the whole time I was struggling to pay for school and was buried under debt. He had it the whole time I stayed an extra two years with Stephanie because I didn't want to have to pay alimony along with my student loans. He had it the whole time I picked up extra shifts to help cover his medical bills at the end."

The controlled tone of his voice slipped away like a Band-Aid coming off to reveal an oozing wound.

"He could have made our lives so much easier and better. I told Jordan that. I told her we should keep the money. No one cared about it now. We weren't hurting anyone by keeping it."

Jordan must have said no.

And Zach must have known his sister well enough to know that time wouldn't change her mind. She was the woman who did the right thing when she found out about a potential drug scandal at her job. She couldn't have known when she started investigating that Papyrus Medical wasn't aware of what Dexter Ruffalo had done. She'd been willing to put her career on the line to right a wrong.

She'd called Otto once she realized that her dad's partner must have been in on it. She'd wanted to give him a chance to do the right thing and confess rather than simply turning the money in and having the police show up on Otto's doorstep, unannounced, with questions again.

She'd probably even opened the door to her brother the day she died, hoping he'd changed his mind and would go with her to take the money to the police.

She'd been a good person. Her main mistake was trusting her brother.

He knew her, but she hadn't known him.

I couldn't defend a man who'd killed someone like that and admitted it and still sounded like he thought he'd done the right thing.

I wouldn't defend a man like that.

"You already figured out the rest," Zach said. "I pocketed the leftover SUX from work. I didn't need much. Then I posed it all to look like a suicide. I obviously didn't understand well enough how much crime scene forensics could tell, or I would have done an even better job."

He stood up and brushed his hands down his pants in a

smoothing motion, almost like he was brushing the whole dirty business away from himself. "One good thing came out of me not telling you all this from the start. You managed to create strong reasonable doubt with Otto Corder. No one will believe Jordan was killed by her brother when she could have been killed by the man who already confessed to two crimes." He stilled. "How's your private investigator doing?"

Nope. I couldn't. He had no right to ask about Hal. Hal was run down by Otto *because* Zach lied to us. Zach had no right to know that the doctors anticipated Hal would have a full recovery. He had no right to pretend that his lies weren't the impetus for everything that happened even if he hadn't been the one behind the wheel.

I moved past Zach and out of my office. I banged on Anderson's door and kept banging until he opened it.

From this moment on, he could deal with Zach Williams.

28

"They denied our petition," Anderson said, static making his voice break up slightly as if he were on the move but not in the car.

Anderson's tone had an edge to it that made me feel like I was talking to my dad when he'd been blocked from doing what he wanted to do.

More static clicked across the line. "They said we're far enough in that changing counsel would unduly bias the jury against Williams. If we renege on our responsibility, we'll be risking a mistrial and costing the taxpayers unnecessary expense."

Anderson's tone made sense now. My parents believed that almost everything was negotiable, and they would argue or bargain until they got their way.

With one exception.

They respected the judge, and in the courtroom, they never broke the rules because it could cost them their case or result in sanctions from the governing body. It wasn't like on *Matlock* when Matlock would sometimes lose his temper and end up in contempt of court and he didn't much care. The courtroom was a professional arena, and my parents believed in maintaining a professional, respected reputation.

"I'll take the case back from you." Anderson's voice had shifted now, like he'd misinterpreted my silence. "I'm the one who told you he was innocent, and I should have noticed that he was lying when I asked him."

Anderson wasn't the one I blamed here. "Zach fooled us both. You had no way of knowing he'd lie to you when you laid out the rule."

Giving the case back to him didn't quite feel right, either, but there wasn't another way to go. We both knew I wouldn't be able to properly represent someone I knew was guilty. My inability to perform when I didn't believe the client should walk free was why I'd been such a failure at my career when I worked for my parents.

I arranged with Anderson to drop off any of the material relating to the case that I still had at my house. I'd planned to swing by and visit Hal anyway. Days in the hospital felt extra-long when you were confined to bed.

I set my phone on my kitchen counter and stared at it.

Anderson was more upset that Zach lied to him than that Zach was guilty. Whether Zach was guilty or not didn't matter to him.

It mattered to me.

Zach had pointed out that I'd provided an amazing alternative explanation for who killed Jordan. Otto was the perfect scapegoat. He had a motive, and thanks to his attack on Hal and me, he had a record of violence.

Anderson would get Zach acquitted.

A key scraped in the door, and Mark came in. Velma barked twice, then she and Toby broke into the happy wiggle-dance that they did when either of us arrived home.

I walked straight into his arms for a hug, not even giving Velma a chance to get in our way.

"Bad day?" Mark asked.

I updated him on the decree. "I guess it's some comfort that I don't have to defend Zach, but I still contributed to him walking free when he should be going to prison. There's not even a loophole where I can expose him as guilty. Everything I know about Jordan's murder is covered under attorney–client privilege."

Mark slid an arm around my waist. "I was planning to surprise you with dinner out tonight, and it seems like you need it now more than ever."

I did. And it was for the best. I'd forgotten to arrange anything for supper anyway.

29

I laid in bed, staring at the ceiling, long after Mark's breathing turned deep and regular.

There weren't any loopholes. My mind kept coming back to that single fact. There weren't any loopholes.

But there had to be a loophole. My parents had taught me that there's always a solution to every problem if you dug hard enough.

I wasn't a Fitzhenry-Dawes for nothing.

I should sleep. We were soon heading into a period in our lives when a good night's sleep might be hard to come by. But it was one thing to know I should sleep and another thing to convince my mind to quiet down long enough to do it.

Prayer didn't work this time. My mind kept reminding me that murder was wrong, and that people who turned a blind eye to murder were guilty. Deep inside me, it felt wrong to walk

away from this. I felt like Pontius Pilate, who washed his hands
and laid Jesus' death at the feet of the angry crowd even though
he had the power to spare Him.

According to professional ethics, I was supposed to keep
quiet. According to my own personal sense of right and wrong,
letting Zach get away with what he'd done was wrong.

Quietly, so as not to wake Mark, I slid out of bed and tiptoed
down the stairs. A whimper came from the direction of the
laundry room and the dogs' crates. I froze. Those two were about
as quiet as a herd of stampeding elephants. If I let them out, there
was no way Mark stayed asleep.

The whimpers died out.

I got an apple from the fridge and headed to the far end of
the kitchen island. Better I put something healthy into my body
than give in to my temptation to stress eat my way through the
entire carton of chocolate chunk ice cream in our freezer. Mark
and I had already had ice cream out after dinner tonight, and
we'd eaten it while walking along the water.

It'd been such a peaceful date night that I almost forgot about
my dilemma.

I turned on the under-the-counter lights. They gave enough
illumination that I could see, but not enough that the dogs would
notice it and think it was morning.

What I needed was a way around the expectation of confidentiality and attorney–client privilege.

The problem was that all the criminal acts Zach had

committed in the past were covered because he told me while I was acting in my capacity as an attorney. Anything that he'd done in the past was covered under privilege.

I'd only be able to report what I knew if it was a future crime. As far as I knew, Zach didn't plan to kill anyone else or rob any more armored cars. Why would he need to? He had more than enough money to live off of thanks to what his dad and Otto stole.

Maybe that was it. Privilege only covered past crimes.

Zach was in possession of stolen goods. He knew the money was stolen, but he kept it anyway. Even if he tried to claim that he didn't know it was stolen, it'd be ruled willful blindness because, with that much money, he should have made inquiries into where it came from. Besides, if he hadn't at least suspected it was stolen, he would have deposited it in the bank. I knew he hadn't since his financial records didn't show any strange trans-actions.

Possession of stolen goods was ongoing criminal activity. If you looked at it the right way, it wasn't covered under privilege. In fact, I had a duty to report if I knew that my client was partici-pating in ongoing criminal activity or planned to commit a crime in the future.

My idea walked a line. Technically, I couldn't share anything that a client told me if the client expected me to keep it a secret. Because this was about an ongoing crime, however, the fact that he'd mentioned having the stolen money during a privileged communication could be considered to circumvent that.

Worst case, I lost my license and Zach walked free anyway. But at least I'd have done everything I could.

If I succeeded, Zach would go to prison for ten years for possession of stolen property. Given the related circumstances, even Anderson might not be able to get him off on the charge of murdering Jordan. Keeping that much stolen money gave him as strong a motive as Otto, and he had access to SUX when Otto didn't.

It might just be enough.

THE NEXT MORNING, I DROPPED OFF THE FILES TO ANDERSON, visited Hal in the hospital, and then I went to the police station in Grand Rapids that had originally investigated the armored car robbery. I didn't tell either Anderson or Hal what I planned to do. Hal didn't need to be thinking about anything work-related, and Anderson would have tried to stop me.

The officer I spoke to hadn't worked the case given how long ago it happened, but he was confident he'd be able to get a warrant to search any property belonging to Zach Williams.

As soon as I left the police station, it felt like I could draw a full breath for the first time in days. I'd done what I could, and it was now out of my hands.

MANDY SENT ME ENOUGH TEXTS AND CALLS THE NEXT FEW DAYS inviting me to everything from trips to the craft store to helping her plan the next month's menu for the Sunburnt Arms. If I didn't know better, I would have thought she knew what I'd done and wanted to make sure I was okay.

I knew for a fact she didn't know. I'd only told Mark, and we'd decided it would be better to keep it between us.

It wasn't the first string of weird behavior from Mandy recently, though. She was definitely up to something. Maybe she and Russ were a couple, and she wanted to tell me, but she kept chickening out.

Though that didn't seem likely. She had no reason to be worried about telling me if that was the case. I wanted them both to be happy. If they'd found happiness with each other, they had my support. Stranger matches had happened.

I was sitting on an upside-down bucket next to Mandy at the local you-pick strawberry place when my phone flashed with Anderson's number.

I'd been sweating from the sun a moment before. Now a chill ran over my arms. He might be calling me for any number of reasons. But my gut told me this call was about what I'd done.

For the first two rings, I considered letting it go to voicemail. Instead, I set my basket aside and answered.

"You could have at least warned me, Nicole."

So much for the possibility that this wasn't about what I'd done. I wouldn't play dumb. I respected Anderson too much for that. "You would have tried to talk me out of it."

"You've got that right." I got the impression that he wanted to swear, but he'd modeled his business enough after my father that he'd probably trained himself not to do that, either. "You still should have come to me. It's one thing to not be able to trust our clients, but we should be able to trust each other."

My head felt hot like it would have if I'd been out in the sun all day without a hat and enough water to drink. I hadn't thought about it that way. Anderson would have tried to stop me. He would have given me all the arguments against it that I'd already walked through in my own mind. He might have even cautioned me about what this might do to the business.

In the end, though, he'd have let me make my own choice. Now he must feel like I'd gone behind his back and I didn't care about how my actions affected him or the business.

I shifted slightly away from Mandy. No doubt she'd eavesdrop anyway, but I didn't need to make it easier for her. "I'm sorry. I didn't think about it that way. I promise it won't happen again."

"We'll be lucky if you get a chance to prove that. Williams is filing a grievance with the Attorney Discipline Board, claiming that you broke both confidentiality and attorney–client privilege."

My heart felt like it had come loose and was spinning out of control in my chest. It'd been a risk I was willing to take. The potential benefit outweighed the potential cost.

Zach wouldn't have filed a grievance if my plan hadn't worked, would he? "The police found the money and arrested him?"

"He's been charged with possession of goods." Anderson drew in a long breath. "The DA felt that you were well within ethical guidelines to report it. I have to agree, so we'll hope the Board sees it the same way. You might get away with a strongly worded reprimand."

My parents would be horrified that I got even that much, but they didn't have the same problems with helping criminals go free that I did. They likely wouldn't even understand why I'd taken the risk. Ideally, they'd never have to find out.

"Is the client retaining you as his lawyer for the possession charge?" I omitted Zach's name since I couldn't be sure how much Mandy or the other people picking strawberries could hear even with keeping my voice low.

Anderson made a negative noise. "He doesn't need to. I convinced him to take a plea deal for both charges."

I rocked back on the basket. There was only one reason Anderson would do something like that when there was any chance that he could still finagle a win. He'd done it because of how upset I was at the thought that Zach would go free for Jordan's murder due to the work I'd done.

"Thank you for that."

"I didn't want to deal with a lying client anymore, anyway."
His tone still said *I'm annoyed at you*, but it'd lessened. "Let me
know when you hear from the Board, alright?"

"I will."

I disconnected the call and tucked my phone into my bag, out
of the sun.

The expression on Mandy's face suggested there was a war
going on inside her. She knew she shouldn't have been eaves-
dropping, but it was killing her not to ask for details on what
she'd overheard.

She didn't need to worry. I was going to tell her the parts
that I was allowed to.

Because all I wanted to do was cry. Cry for Jordan, who had
so much good left to give the world. Cry for Otto and for Hank
Williams that they'd made a bad choice that changed the course
of their lives and their children's lives. Cry for the situation I'd
created with Anderson. He'd been understanding, but what I'd
done would put a mark on our firm's reputation.

I'd done the right thing, but that didn't mean there wouldn't
be consequences. Intellectually knowing there might be consequences and realistically having to face them were sometimes
two different things.

Pregnancy hormones probably lay at the bottom of the urge
to cry, but my desire to sit in the hot sun and pick strawberries
had vanished.

I met Mandy's gaze. "I'll tell you about it in the car, but can we go home now?"

Her upper body leaned toward me like she wanted to reach out and put an arm around me, but that strange look flashed across her face again. She stretched a hand out toward my half-empty basket. "Don't you think we should finish? I'm willing to wait to hear about what's going on until we're somewhere more private. It'd be a shame not to finish."

She was willing to wait? That was the most un-Mandy like statement ever. Now I was sure there was something going on, and it wasn't merely my latent paranoia.

I'd already picked a basket and a half. That was enough for us to eat fresh or have on ice cream and to make the strawberry bread recipe that Mandy had promised me as part of my ongoing quest to be able to bake a few simple items before the baby was old enough to eat solid food.

I kept my expression neutral. Until I knew what was happening, I didn't want to let on that I suspected anything. "I have enough with what I've picked." I inclined my head toward Mandy's baskets. In the same amount of time, she'd managed to pick three times as many as I had. I'd cut off that excuse before she tried it. "And that looks like what you said you needed for your first batches of jam."

She'd talked the whole way here about how many trips to the you-pick she normally made in a summer because one of the

Sunburnt Arms' draws over the competition was their home-made local jams.

Her eyes shifted left then right, as if she were looking for some other way to distract me. "Well, then, why don't you come back with me? I'll teach you how to make jam. I know you said you'd never want store-bought jam again after trying mine."

She almost had me. I did want to learn how to make jam. The jam I could get at the store tasted like sugar. Her jam tasted like sweet fruit.

Unfortunately for her, the more she tried to convince me not to go home, the more I wanted to know why. "I'm too tired today. I'd just like to head back and take a nap."

"We have beds," Mandy blurted.

I locked my gaze on her. She looked everywhere other than at me.

"Is there something you need to tell me?" I asked.

She shook her head and gathered up her baskets without another objection.

At the checkout counter, she changed her mind twice about whether or not pay with cash or credit card. She finally chose cash and counted the amount out twice.

While I was paying for mine, she pulled her phone out of her purse and sent a text. The frantic way she tapped the screen made me think it had something to do with me wanting to head home early.

Something had to be going on at my house that Mandy didn't want me to know about.

It couldn't be a surprise baby shower. She and Stacey planned to throw me one closer to my due date, and we were too early to even start planning that one. Besides, I'd made it clear to everyone—I thought—how much I hated surprises.

Mandy drove back to Sugarwood so slowly that a turtle would have honked his horn at us.

Her delay tactics made it seem like she was trying to buy time. For someone to get out of my house, or for someone to finish something in my house?

A car I didn't recognize parked behind my car and Mark's truck in our driveway. Mark had planned to do some paperwork from home today, and he hadn't mentioned that anyone was coming over. He was a terrible liar, but maybe he was good at omission.

The front door opened as soon as I climbed out of the car.

Mark met me partway down the sidewalk and took the strawberry baskets from my arms. He didn't look guilty the way Mandy did. It was more like he was about to face something he'd expected was coming but had hoped to put off.

"Is there any way I can convince you not to poke around inside right now?" he asked.

"I didn't tell her anything, I swear," Mandy's words came out in a hiss as if she thought that way only Mark could understand.

She was out of luck. Mark wasn't a snake, and she didn't speak Parseltongue like in *Harry Potter*.

First my parents and now Mandy and Mark. I get pregnant, and everyone starts sneaking around behind my back. Being pregnant didn't make me any less capable or competent or intelligent than I'd been before.

But the part nervous, part excited look on Mark's face told me that whatever they were up to wasn't going to be any worse than my parents hiring Hal to take care of me. If Hal hadn't been with me the day Otto tried to run us down, I'd likely be dead. Or I'd have lost the baby.

Mark linked his fingers with mine and led me up the stairs. Mandy trailed along behind us. If she were anyone else, I'd have said her tagging along was another clue that whatever I'd find upstairs was a good thing. With Mandy, it didn't mean anything except that she didn't want to miss the chance for a good story.

The door to the baby's room hung open even though we normally kept it closed since it wasn't a used room at present. My theory had always been that closed rooms collected less dust and therefore had to be dusted less often.

Mark moved to the side, giving me a full view of the inside of the room.

A mural filled with elephants, giraffes, zebras, hippopotamuses, and a plethora of other colorful zoo animals and trees covered two of the walls. A woman in her late twenties, her hair covered by a kerchief, a paint palette in one hand and a brush in the other, stood by the third wall. Shapes covered the wall behind her, outlining where the rest of the mural would appear once she finished.

A light breeze filtered through the room from the open windows.

My brain couldn't put together a full, clear sentence. This was what Mandy and Mark had been scheming about for the past few weeks. It had to be why Mandy seemed nervous that day that I called and told her I had a theory. She thought I'd figured out about the mural. That explained why she relaxed when I told her someone had hired Hal to follow me around. She knew their secret was still safe.

"I wanted it to be finished before you saw it," Mark said, "but we knew there was a chance you'd find out ahead of time."

This also explained why Mandy had been monopolizing my time the past few days. That must have been when the painter started her work in the house. Inviting me to everything imaginable was the only way they could guarantee where I'd be and how long I'd be gone. I'd thrown a kink into it today by wanting to come home early.

"How long have you two been planning this?" I couldn't quite keep the shell-shocked tone out of my voice. Everywhere I looked I felt like I was seeing something new. The way she'd played with colors and depth—I wouldn't have imagined it was possible on a two-dimensional surface.

"It was Mark's idea." Mandy edged a little closer, like she

wanted a peek into how the room was coming along, too. She wouldn't have seen it yet, either, having spent so much time with me as a cover. "I just enlisted my goddaughter to help and gave her a place to stay while she's here since she lives in Detroit."

The woman in the kerchief waved the hand holding the paintbrush. "Audrey. I love your dogs."

Mark moved in behind me and wrapped his arms around me. "Do you like it? It should work for either a boy or a girl."

"I see how it is." I elbowed him gently in the stomach. I couldn't bring myself to stop looking at the walls. "This is all an attempt to get me to give in about knowing the baby's gender."

"No." I felt Mark smile against my hair. "But did it work?"

I turned around in his arms and brushed a kiss against his lips. "I guess it did."

Maybe I didn't hate *all* surprises. Once in a while, they could be good. After all, this baby had been a surprise, and I already loved him or her.

LETTER FROM THE AUTHOR

I've said it before, but I feel like I can't say it enough. Thank you for coming along on this journey with me, Nicole, Mark, and everyone else in Fair Haven (and surrounding areas).

Nicole and Mark couldn't agree on whether or not to find out their baby's gender, which means we all get to guess until the baby is born. If you have a guess about both the baby's gender and what they'll name him or her, be sure to let me know! You can email me at authoremilyjames@gmail.com. Put "Baby Guess" in the subject line.

The next book, *Stumped*, will be coming out this winter. If you haven't yet signed up for my newsletter, please do. I announce new releases there first. I share recipes and other exclusives. And I give my newsletter subscribers a free ebook copy of *Sapped*, a Maple Syrup Mysteries prequel.

You can sign up at www.smarturl.it/emilyjames.

Love,

Emily

ABOUT THE AUTHOR

Emily James grew up watching TV shows like *Matlock*, *Monk*, and *Murder She Wrote*. (It's pure coincidence that they all begin with an M.) It was no surprise to anyone when she turned into a mystery writer.

Alongside being a writer, she's also a wife, an animal lover, and a new artist. She likes coffee and painting and drinking coffee while painting. She also enjoys cooking. She tries not to do that while painting because, well, you shouldn't eat paint.

Emily and her husband share their home with a blue Great Dane, seven cats (all rescues), and a budgie (who is both the littlest and the loudest).

If you'd like to know as soon as Emily's next mystery releases, please join her newsletter list at www.smarturl.it/emilyjames.

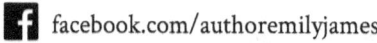 facebook.com/authoremilyjames